"Close the door," Meg said

Even half submerged in warm bathwater, she was shivering from the cold air on her wet skin…and Jack's unexpected presence.

He kicked the bathroom door closed, leaving them in velvet darkness. He drew Meg out of the tub and held her close, enfolding her in his heat, heedless of the water soaking into his clothes.

She knew it was wrong. She shouldn't let him stroke her wet hair and run his big, hot hand down her spine. But it was dark and her senses were filled with him—she longed for his touch, the heady masculine scent of him, the feel of her breasts crushed against his chest, the warmth and the rhythm of his heart. "We…we shouldn't…" she protested weakly.

"Shh…" He pressed her head to his chest and she allowed herself to relax against him.

"It'll never be any other way between us, Meg. We'll never stop needing each other."

He was right. It would always be like this between them. And she couldn't hope to hide her response. Not even in the dark.

Pamela Burford loves combining toe-curling romance with the thrill of suspense and mystery. This time she added a far-out family and a stunning secret, and the result was *Jacks Are Wild*. A rising star, Pamela won first place in the Heart of the West national writing contest with her first Temptation novel, *A Hard-Hearted Hero*. With her identical twin sister, Patricia Ryan, she went on to complete a cross-series collaboration between Intrigue and Temptation, which has received rave reviews. Pam lives on Long Island with her husband and two children, and is president and founder of Long Island Romance Writers. She loves to hear from readers: P.O. Box 1321, North Baldwin, NY 11510-0721. (Please send an SASE for a reply.)

Books by Pamela Burford

HARLEQUIN TEMPTATION
644—A HARD-HEARTED HERO

HARLEQUIN INTRIGUE
360—HIS SECRET SIDE
420—TWICE BURNED (Double Dare)

JACKS ARE WILD
Pamela Burford

Harlequin Books

TORONTO • NEW YORK • LONDON
AMSTERDAM • PARIS • SYDNEY • HAMBURG
STOCKHOLM • ATHENS • TOKYO • MILAN
MADRID • WARSAW • BUDAPEST • AUCKLAND

To my daughter, Rebecca,
who served as unwitting model
for the youngest characters in this story.

ISBN 0-373-25758-9

JACKS ARE WILD

Copyright © 1997 by Pamela Burford Loeser.

1

"WHAT THE HE—heck are *you* doing here?"

Meg Wolf censored her tongue for the sake of the six tiny ears attached to three cherubic faces lighting up at the sight of her ex-husband. Uncle Pete's living room had just gotten a lot smaller.

"Daddy!" Five-year-old Nora charged full tilt at Jack Wolf, who neatly caught her up and swung her around. Jack perched her on one lean hip, her little bottom supported by a long arm ropy from hard work. He bent to scoop up seven-year-old Marie on the other side while three-year-old Daisy hopped and whined, chubby arms raised imploringly.

"Just a second, angel, gotta unload some cargo first." He let Nora slide to the floor. Giggling, she clawed at his T-shirt in a futile attempt to hold her ground.

The red-and-black shirt was emblazoned with the words *Wolf Mann Brew Pub, Ithaca, New York*, in a bold, distinctive design Meg had never seen before. Had he and his partner, Kevin Mann, hired a graphic artist? She wondered how he could afford such a luxury, knowing the child-support payments he sent every month had to eat up most of his income. It didn't sit right with her, taking his money when she was certain she now earned much more than he did. The thought briefly crossed her mind that he might try to have the payments lowered.

No. He'd never do that. His innate pride and sense of honor wouldn't let him.

Jack's teasing grin never faltered as he glanced at Meg, but she saw something flicker in his light blue eyes. Wariness. Caution. As if he was mentally assessing just how twisted her knickers were getting over this blatant breach of divorce protocol.

"What a *surprise* to see Daddy here, huh, girls?" She crossed her arms over her chest. Jack smirked at her syrupy tone.

Nora said, "I didn't know you were gonna be here, Daddy!"

"We're gonna have Thanksgiving with Daddy!" crowed Marie. She hugged her father harder and pulled back to rub his beard stubble. "You're scratchy."

Meg groaned inwardly as she took in the girls' beaming faces. Damn Jack. Damn him for teasing them with his presence, raising their expectations.

"Daddy's just here to wish us a happy holiday, girls. *He can't stay*," she said, with a meaningful glare at the daddy in question.

Three little faces fell. Meg felt like Cruella de Ville. Trust her ex to cast *her* as the heavy.

He said, "Not so fast, Mommy. As a matter of fact, I will be sharing that turkey with my favorite gals. I'm getting a whole four days with you."

Meg had to shout to be heard over the delighted

squeals. "Uncle Pete invited you?" That was impossible. Pete detested Jack! He'd never have invited him to his annual Turkey Day get-together at his island vacation home.

Jack's eyes slid away. "Not exactly."

She should have guessed. "Tanya. You wheedled an invitation out of Tanya."

He met her gaze now as he lowered his daughters to the braided rug. "She invited me. No one did any wheedling."

She smirked, well aware that Pete's wife had her own agenda where Jack was concerned.

"I want to see my daughters, Meg. I want to spend Thanksgiving with them. Is that too much to ask? Just one holiday together—"

"Girls, go upstairs and choose your beds. Marie, do you remember what room? Last one on this side?" she asked, pointing to the horseshoe-shaped hallway that overlooked the living room, a wooden balustrade running its length. Her oldest daughter nodded, and Meg forced a smile. "Good. I want Daisy in a lower bunk. I'll be up in a few minutes."

The girls pounded up the stairs, blond curls bouncing. She turned on Jack. "Just what do you think you're doing?"

"I told you, I was invit—"

"By that—that..." She glanced around quickly and lowered her voice. "That bimbo!"

Jack chuckled. "Is that any way to speak about your aunt?"

"She's not my aunt, she's the shameless gold digger who managed to rope my uncle Pete into marriage."

"Meg." He took a step toward her. She crossed her arms again and he stopped, with a weary little sigh. "Come on. It's Thanksgiving. I don't want to spend the next few days tussling with you. I just want to see my little girls. For more than a few hours this time."

"You're setting them up for disappointment, Jack. They'll expect this to be a regular thing."

He just looked at her for long moments. Finally he murmured, "Would that be so bad?"

His forlorn expression, the mingled hope and pain she read there, pierced her like a knife. She struggled to put starch in her words, in her resolve. *Remember*, she commanded herself. *Remember why you left him.*

"I'm afraid I can't allow this," she said.

A muscle jumped in his cheek. "I'm afraid you have no choice. I'm an invited guest and I'm staying."

"We'll see about—"

"That boat ride was murder!"

Startled, Jack swung his gaze to the front door and the dapper, dark-haired stranger hauling two designer suitcases through it. One look at Meg's face was all Jack needed. He swore under his breath.

The man set down his luggage and cast a quick and approving glance at the high-ceilinged room, with its dark paneling, enormous stone fireplace and ponderous leather furniture. "You were right, darling. This place is charming!" He wore a tweed sport coat over a blue, oxford-cloth shirt, with knife-creased gray slacks and gleaming loafers. His neatly trimmed dark hair sported a touch of gray at the temples.

Meg licked her lips and twisted a strand of pale blond hair around a finger. Jack almost smiled. Some things never changed.

The boyfriend droned on, "It reminds me of the cottage on the Cape where my people used to summer." Noticing Jack, he stepped forward and thrust out his hand.

"D. Winston Kent. I'm Meg's fiancé."

A huge iron ball slammed into Jack's chest. In the space of a heartbeat a thousand thoughts assailed him, one paramount among them.

It's really over.

He forced his eyes to focus on D. Winston Kent's genial expression and the manicured hand extended toward him, forced his overloaded mind to catch up and do what was expected.

He was a man. He'd act like one. He wouldn't shame himself. Or Meg.

Jack raised his hand and clasped the other man's smooth palm. "Jack Wolf," he said. "What's the *D* stand for?"

The firm handclasp stalled in midpump. D. Winston Kent's dark brown eyes widened. He looked at Meg, who was staring into space, twirling that lock of hair to beat the band. Only then did Jack notice the square-shaped diamond on her ring finger. The thing was the size of a Chiclet.

That was the finger on which he'd once lovingly, proudly, placed a wedding band. At the time, he couldn't afford a diamond, but he'd always meant to make up for that lapse someday.

"It...stands for Donald," her fiancé said at last, pasting a wooden smile on his clean-shaven face. "Actually, it's Donald Winston Kent the Third. But call me Winston."

"Well, I'm more a one-of-a-kind guy myself, Winston. Somehow I don't think any of my daughters would have appreciated being called Jack Junior." Was that a proprietary spin he gave to "my daughters"? *My* daughters?

Meg said, "Winston, I, uh, hadn't realized Uncle Pete's wife invited Jack this weekend." She shoved her hands in the pockets of her windbreaker and addressed Jack. "Now you see why it's not a good idea for you to stay."

"Nonsense." Winston slid an arm around her stiff shoulders. "Jack and I have to get acquainted sooner or later. Might as well be sooner." He seemed oblivious to the nonverbal signals his ladylove was pelting him with, easily interpreted as *stay the hell out of this.* Blithely he droned on, "It's just as we discussed, darling. The girls should see us all getting along, in order to fully internalize the reality of their new family—"

"Winston..."

"—and gain a healthy sense of closure."

A surge in his blood pressure nearly boosted Jack off his feet. Meg looked like she'd just been handed a blindfold and a cigarette. Wearing a smug little smile, Winston gave her shoulder a hearty squeeze.

Jack spoke just one word, as soft and low as a panther's warning growl. "Closure?"

"Winston!" Smiling brightly—too brightly—Meg disengaged herself from her fiancé's arm. "Why don't you take the bags upstairs? Your room is the middle one, right there." She pointed. "You'll be sharing it with my cousin Neal."

"Certainly. I'll check on the kids, make sure they're getting settled in okay." He lifted the bags, nodded to Jack and made his way up the curving staircase and down the hall.

Meg bit her lip. "I didn't mean for you to find out like this."

"Winston Kent, Meg?" Jack couldn't bear the way she was looking at him, the gentle sympathy underlying her words. "Winston? Kent?" he sneered.

Her delicate, dimpled chin jutted and angry color flooded her cheeks. *Good.*

"Who were the runners-up?" he asked. "Raleigh Chesterfield? Benson Hedges? Joe Camel?"

"Trust you to respond with typical maturity."

"Meg, the man uses *summer* as a verb."

She blushed harder. "Don't expect me to apologize for Winston's privileged background."

"What does he do for a living?"

"He's a partner at Watkins, Gilroy and Stone."

Something shriveled deep within Jack. The bastard had a piece of one of Wall Street's most prestigious law firms. This was the kind of husband Meg had always wanted, the kind of husband she'd tried to turn Jack into for five years.

"A little long in the tooth for you, no?" he asked. "What is he, forty? Forty-two?"

She shrugged. "Something like that."

"*Something* like that?"

She rolled her eyes. "Forty-five."

"Forty-*five*? For God's sake, Meg, you're only twenty-seven. That's a difference of—"

"I can do the math."

"What are you doing with a forty-five-year-old guy?" He allowed himself a mirthless chuckle. "Silly question. Is he any good?"

"Go to hell."

He was already there. "Do you love him?"

She blinked. "What kind of question is that?"

"Just...wondering." *Go ahead, it won't kill you.* "I wish you well, Meg. I want you to know that."

She searched his expression, her own tightly shuttered. "Thank you."

He took a deep breath. "So. How's it been, working for Pete? I hope he treats his employees better than his relatives."

"I can't complain. He just promoted me to VP of marketing."

"Congratulations. You get another hefty raise out of it?"

"Uh, yeah."

She seemed embarrassed by that, foolish woman. Probably thought her ex-husband was living hand-to-mouth.

Meg looked as uptight as Jack felt. He had to escape. Just a few moments alone to sort out his thoughts, regroup—and come to terms with the finality that he could no longer avoid.

"Listen, I, uh, brought some beer. I have to go and stick it in the fridge·or it won't be cold for—"

"I've got stuff to do, too." She waved him away with a tense little smile.

He made his way to the pantry off the kitchen, where he'd left the three cases of beer that he'd brought from the brew pub as a peace offering for his host. He slit open the cardboard with his pocketknife and began stacking bottles in the emptier of the two refrigerators.

Now that it was over—for good—he couldn't help pondering how far he and Meg had come from their first bizarre encounter eight years ago.

That year, spring never arrived in upstate New York. A sudden heat wave rolled in on the heels of the last April snow flurries. The day Jack met Meg, the mercury hovered close to eighty and the sky was a blinding azure. Out of boredom he'd accepted Gus Black's invitation to a daylong barbecue party at the house Gus shared with seven other students, near the State University at Binghamton.

The dilapidated house and grounds were overrun with students in high spirits, celebrating the brief reprieve between winter inertia and cramming for finals. The prevailing mood ranged from giddy to downright raucous.

One girl stood out. Jack had noticed the pretty blond freshman around campus during the school year, bundled against the elements, hauling her backpack of books between buildings. Now he finally got to see what the heavy parka had concealed—a lovely, graceful body in frayed cutoffs and a sleeveless black T-shirt.

His practiced eye instantly discerned what a less observant fellow might have missed at first glance. Her small breasts, youthfully high and firm, were unencumbered by a bra. Only the most subtle sway and quiver of soft flesh gave it away. You had to look hard.

God, he loved the first signs of spring.

The party was a dud. Jack knew it within the first fifteen minutes. As a twenty-four-year-old sophomore, he had little in common with his fellow students. At the moment he felt downright ancient, depressed by their relentless, manic joviality, fueled by liberal quantities of booze. He'd outgrown that brand of juvenile excess when most of these kids were in grade school. As for the little huddles he spotted in odd corners and behind half-closed doors, it didn't take a genius to figure out what was going on there.

Deciding he had better ways to spend this glorious day, he mumbled some excuse to Gus, who was preoccupied with emptying a pitcher of beer over another youth's head. Jack was circling the house, heading for his battered, secondhand Jeep, when he heard it—a female voice, shrill and affronted. And scared. A breathless hitch inflected her words when she told whoever she was with to get his hands the hell off her.

He recognized that voice. It was the blonde, the girl called Meg. He also recognized the inebriated snicker that answered her, though the words that followed were muffled by a clump of overgrown junipers that concealed the pair. It was Drew Haley, one of Gus's housemates. A big, blond senior whose credo was Better Living through Chemistry. His nickname was Fog.

The decision to intercede hadn't been a conscious one, more a reflex action. In the next moment Jack was staring into Fog's unnaturally wide pupils. Meg's lips were the same shade of white as her face. Fog's beefy hand shackled her upper arm in a bruising grip.

The altercation that followed was brief, the outcome predictable. Jack didn't question his ability to intimidate. It was a skill he'd honed in the most demanding arena imaginable, where survival and sanity depended on making men fear you. This blustering dopehead never had a chance. Jack turned the man's bowels to jelly without raising his voice.

Afterward Jack escorted Meg back to her dorm, where he met her moon-faced, dulcimer-strumming roommate and her striped cat named Trout. They shared a bottle of too sweet liebfraumilch and grilled cheese sandwiches made with an electric iron, and he watched her blush and twist her hair when he scrutinized her portfolio of watercolors. They were good and he told her so.

He managed to hold out till their third date before going for the gold. She pried his busy hands out of her jeans and said no. *I've never*, she said. *Can you wait?*

He kissed her tenderly. *I can wait*, he told her. *It's okay.*

It wasn't okay. He was frustrated as hell.

But he was pleased, too.

Eight long months later, during Christmas break, they made love on the fold-out couch in his studio apartment. Snow pattered softly on the windowpanes as he inhaled her sharp gasp, as overcome as she by the newness and wonder of it. As if it were his first time, too.

In a way, it had been.

Jack leaned on the open refrigerator door now, staring at shelves full of brown and green bottles, but seeing Meg's face as she'd looked a few minutes ago. Inflexible. Wary.

Was this the same grateful, ingenuous girl who, only half teasing, had called him her white knight as they drove away from that horrendous party eight years ago?

Was this the same strong, brave woman who'd clutched his hand and cursed him soundly as she struggled to bring his babies into the world? After each birth the two of them had wept and laughed and said, "Let's do it again."

What had happened to that woman? To the bond they'd shared, the vows they'd exchanged?

Part of the blame lay with her uncle Pete, who'd schemed to break them up almost from the beginning; it was some sort of power trip for him. He'd constantly urged Meg to leave Jack and take a lucrative job with his company in Queens, always laying it on thickest when she was at her most vulnerable, when the checking account was depleted and she was worn-out from the kids and worried about the future.

If Jack had thought he could have kept her by sacrificing his dream, by remaking himself as the nine-to-five drone she'd always wanted him to be, he might have done it. Only he knew, as she couldn't, that it wouldn't have been enough. Eventually she'd have discovered the truth about him, the ugly past he'd never been able to bring himself to share with her, despite his best intentions, despite his gnawing need to expose it, exorcise it.

Sooner or later she'd have found out who and what she'd married, and it would have been the final blow no matter how many concessions he'd made to middle-class stability.

The hell of it was, he'd been all prepared to tell her this weekend, just to get it out in the open. Damn the consequences.

He'd even allowed himself to harbor the foolish hope that his stunning admission might actually prove to be cathartic, a sort of electroshock therapy to jump-start their relationship and get them talking again. He'd half convinced himself this brief holiday together would be a turning point. The first step toward reconciliation.

He shoved the last bottle of beer in the fridge and slammed the door. Hard. Sounded like a giant wind chime in there.

Yep, he'd been all set to win back his wife and children. A big man with big plans. Only he hadn't counted on Meg having a few plans of her own.

And a new white knight by the name of D. Winston Kent III.

Esquire.

2

JACK PAUSED at the entrance to the living room to watch his ex-wife sift through a red plastic tote basket filled with the girls' travel toys. The woman even looked sexy sorting crayons and markers.

"Meg! Hi!"

They both looked up at the chirpy greeting to see Tanya Stanton leaning over the second-floor railing. She wore sprayed-on black jeans and a loose pink V-neck sweater that had slipped off a shoulder, revealing a black bra strap. The necklaces dripping into her cleavage were without a doubt pure gold. Her hair was big and platinum blond. Last time Jack had seen her it had been red.

She leaned farther over the railing, stretching the sweater and revealing even more of the bounty spilling from her Marvel bra. Somehow Jack didn't think the display was for Meg's benefit.

Tanya stage-whispered, "That Winston is *adorable*, Meg! Do you know he's in there helping your little girls unpack and setting out their little shoes and toothbrushes and hair things all in neat little rows, lined up just so? He's just *adorable!*"

Meg glanced nervously at Jack. With great strength

of will he took a deep breath and unclenched his fists. Damned if he'd let her see him lose his cool.

Tanya started down the stairs, negligently straightening her sweater's neckline, which simply slid off the other shoulder. "How was the boat ride over, Meg?"

"Choppy. The wind has picked up and I don't like the way the sky looks. The *Mermaid* will return on Sunday around noon to take us back."

Jack ran a hand over his stubbly, unshaven jaw and pushed a few errant, light brown curls off his forehead. He wished he'd had time to make himself presentable before seeing Meg and the girls, but Tanya, with typical foresight, hadn't invited him till late last night.

He'd been putting in long hours at the Wolf Mann Brew Pub, longer hours than his partner, Kevin Mann, who had a wife at home. The frantic pace of the early years had slacked off; the pub was in the black and they'd hired dependable, trustworthy help who knew how to keep the place running in their absence.

But Jack preferred the cheerfully hectic ambience of the pub to his own brooding company at home. So he spent sixteen hours a day there, supervising brewing and other business in the mornings and overseeing pub traffic until 1:00 a.m., when he locked up.

That didn't leave much time for niceties like regular haircuts, and what did it matter how shaggy he looked? Kevin didn't care. And as far as his customers were concerned, a touch of grunge only enhanced his image as a maverick independent brewmaster.

But then came Tanya's call, with the invitation to

spend the long Thanksgiving weekend with her and
Pete—and Meg and his little girls. Jack had known it
wouldn't sit well with Meg, but he figured he'd worry
about that when he got there. He'd asked Kevin to
cover for him, thrown some clothes into his beat-up
duffel, swung by the pub for the beer and driven all
night from Ithaca down to eastern Long Island.

With his foot to the floor, he'd just made the 7:00
a.m. departure of the boat the Stantons had chartered
to take the family to the small private island that had
been in Pete's family for four generations. Meg and
the kids were taking a later boat. Naturally, Tanya had
failed to mention that Meg was bringing her fiancé. A
deliberate oversight, no doubt. Pete had been furious
to see Jack, of course, but Tanya had managed to calm
him down. If there was one thing Tanya excelled at, it
was manipulating men.

The lady now lingered at the bottom of the stairs,
where she struck what she no doubt considered an alluring pose. Jack tore his gaze from the spectacle and
caught Meg's eye. Just for an instant. Long enough for
them to read each other's minds. As one, they turned
from their hostess and bit their lips to keep from
chuckling. It was a bittersweet moment, a reminder of
the wordless bond they'd once shared.

Tanya's response to the lack of attention was an eloquent sigh. "Well...I better go check on that turkey."
She ambled out of the room.

A moment later her bloodcurdling scream made
Jack's heart leap into his throat.

"Stay back!" He shoved Meg behind him protectively as they charged into the kitchen.

Tanya stood frozen, her bulging eyes focused on what her husband was doing to the bird of honor. Pete Stanton, stogie clamped firmly between his teeth, held a propane torch, its blue flame directed at the paper pouch of giblets still crammed into the turkey's nether regions.

He plucked the cigar from his mouth and announced in his snide nasal drawl, "Son of a bitch is still frozen!" When it came to attitude, Meg's uncle could give lessons to Jack Nicholson. "Bet I could cook the whole damn thing this way, whaddya think?"

The aromas of charred turkey and smoldering paper overwhelmed even the stench of Pete's cigar. Jack was dumbfounded as to why a man who could afford truckloads of Dunhills would willingly smoke stinky bargain cigars. Then again, knowing Pete, he probably did it simply to get on everyone's nerves.

"What are you doing to my turkey?" Tanya shrieked. She was scarlet from her impressive décolletage right up to the dusky roots of her hair. A vein bulged in her neck.

Pete set his stogie on the edge of the sink, his garish diamond pinky ring winking with the movement. He turned down the torch and held the turkey's blackened hind end under a stream of cold water, then jammed his beefy fingers into it. With a savage twist and a mighty pull, he freed the half-frozen giblet bag and tossed it into the sink.

"Voilà." He picked up his cigar, noticed it had gone out, turned up the propane torch and relit it.

"Get out!" Tanya said. "I'll finish this."

"You?" Pete cackled. "This sucker isn't one of your Lite Time entrées, sweetheart. It won't fit in the microwave." Tapping his ash onto the tiled floor, he announced to all present, "Last time I left my wife alone with a turkey, she cooked the damn thing with the whatchacallits—giblets still in it!"

Meg, ever the diplomat, said, "Tanya and I will stuff this bird and get it in the oven. You guys scat! Both of you." She picked up a kitchen towel and snapped it hard at her uncle's ample butt.

"Ow!" On his way out the door he called back to Meg, "You're the only gal with grit enough to stand up to me, you know that? That's why I hired you."

"And stay out if you want to eat." She slammed the door.

Back in the living room, Jack found himself alone with his host for the first time. He despised being an unwelcome guest. Despised the way Pete was looking at him, as if he were something that had crawled up from the beach.

It was a look Jack knew all too well. And it still made him feel like the poor, scrappy kid he'd once been, his pride savaged by constant reminders that he wasn't good enough to share the same planet with guys like Pete Stanton.

Now here he was, thirty-two years old and a business owner—okay, part owner—and he still wasn't

good enough for this meddling, self-important bastard.

So why bother? Why put himself through this?

But he knew why. For his daughters. To spend four
whole days with them. Even if it meant watching their
mother cozy up with her fiancé.

If it weren't for Tanya's invitation, he'd be spending
Thanksgiving alone at home, washing down a turkey
sandwich from the deli with a bottle of...

Let's see—an ale would be too heavy. Some kind of
lager. Jack mentally snapped his fingers. An Oktober-
fest, redolent of rich toasted malt. Not too sweet, and
aromatic enough to stand up to tangy rye bread without overpowering the turkey.

"What the hell's got you so damn goo-goo eyed,
Wolf? A second ago you looked mad enough to spit."
Nobody could sneer like Pete Stanton. He settled into
an easy chair and reached across the lamp table to pull
a huge crystal ashtray closer.

"Beer."

"Huh." Pete's bushy salt-and-pepper eyebrows
pulled together as he worked the stogie to the other
side of his mouth.

Jack picked up a smaller ashtray, crossed to the fireplace and leaned back against the cool stonework.
Digging into his jeans pocket, he pulled out a small
cellophane pack of sunflower seeds—his addiction of
choice for the past seven years, since he gave up ciga-
rettes. Not as satisfying, but certainly healthier. When
Marie was born and he'd looked into her sweet blue

eyes for the first time, he'd decided then and there that he wanted to live to see his grandchildren.

Pete now looked downright "goo-goo eyed" himself. All it took was the mention of beer. Jack was well aware that Pete didn't want to like anything about his favorite niece's ex-husband, but he couldn't help himself. Pete's arrogance might scream old money, but he was as nouveau riche as they came, with tastes to match. No delicately perfumed chardonnays for him. He'd been weaned on Pabst Blue Ribbon.

The man liked beer.

Jack's expertise on that wondrous subject—its history, its endless varieties, even how to make the golden elixir—commanded respect. And that irked the hell out of Pete.

Though he'd made millions from Murder Won, the gritty, bestselling board game in which the aim was not to solve murders but to commit them, Pete's taste in beer remained on a par with his taste in tobacco. He cheerfully swigged can after can of the thin, pale, fizzy lagers that, until the recent microbrewery revolution, were all that was available to American beer drinkers. What Kevin liked to call lawn-mowing beer.

Pete's craggy smirk couldn't disguise the interested glimmer in his eyes. He gesticulated with the moist, masticated cigar stub. "You bring anything halfway decent from that fairy-mary beer bar of yours?"

Jack made a show of examining a black-and-white sunflower seed with its fine patina of salt. He raised it to his mouth and cracked the shell between his molars, relishing the familiar explosion of taste—salt, followed by the nutty sweetness of the seed. He placed the bits of shell in the ashtray.

"Ah, just drop the damn things," Pete said. "Tanya'll sweep 'em up later."

"She's busy enough getting dinner ready."

"Tanya's never busy enough. She's got too much time on her hands. That's what gets gals into trouble. Don't you think?"

Jack paused with a seed halfway to his mouth, transfixed by the chilly flatness of Pete's stare. His nape prickled with the need to steer the conversation to safer ground. "I brought three mixed cases, about a dozen varieties of beer."

"Huh."

"There's a nice dark Christmas ale—goes well with something heavy like a beef stew or pot roast. And a couple of bottles of cream stout. You like stout?"

"Never tried it. Looks like mud. Smells like burnt mud."

"You'll like this stuff. It's got shoulders. You can mix it with a lager to make a black-and-tan, but I like it straight with a salami-onion-and-cheddar sandwich. Wholegrain bread. Plenty of brown mustard."

"What are you, Martha Stewart? I don't give a crap what kinda food it goes with. Just tell me about the damn beer!"

Jack did. And by the time he was finished, his host looked parched.

"That stuff cold yet?"

"Nope."

"Too bad." Pete hauled himself out of his chair and

made a beeline for the pantry. Jack didn't bother to remind him that it wasn't even noon yet.

"Look at Daisy, Daddy!"

He looked up to the second-floor railing, where little Daisy stood between her older sisters, gingerly touching her new hairdo. Her golden curls had been swept up and secured on the top of her head with a plastic barrette shaped like a teddy bear. The straggling bottom strands were bound by two mismatched hair ties. She looked preposterous.

"You look beautiful, angel," he said. "Real fancy. As pretty as Mommy."

She grinned. "I look like Mommy!"

"Can we do your hair, Daddy?" Marie pleaded.

"We'll make a ponytail," Nora offered. "A little one. You got a lotta hair now."

"*Two* ponytails!" Daisy squealed. "Like me."

"Uh...I have to go out and...do something for Uncle Pete." He started edging toward the door. "Mommy's in the kitchen. I bet she could use some help cooking Thanksgiving dinner."

The three little girls whooped and charged down the stairs. Marie and Daisy ran into the kitchen, but Nora hung back. Jack's middle child was the worrier, the deep thinker. At five she'd already engaged her parents in exhaustive discussions of death, justice and the moral ramifications of tattling.

"What is it, sweetheart?" He knelt. She took a hesitant step toward him. "Nora...?"

"Mr. Kent's gonna be our new daddy."

Don't lose it. Jack mentally chanted those three

words in a silent litany of restraint, though it was hard to hear the command over the slamming din of his pulse. When he could speak calmly, he asked, "Did Mommy tell you that?"

"Uh-uh. Mr. Kent did. Is it true, Daddy? I don't want it to be true. I don't want you to stop being my daddy." She bit her quivering bottom lip.

He opened his arms and she ran into them. Let herself be swaddled in the cocoon of his unconditional love.

"I'll always be your daddy," he whispered into her fine, warm hair, inhaling the mingled scents of baby shampoo and little girl. His eyes stung. "*Always*. Nothing is ever going to change that. Okay?"

She clung to him with savage tenacity, his sweet, skinny little Nora, all arms and legs and elbows and knees. At last she pulled back. She nodded, her blue eyes solemn. "Okay." She followed her sisters into the kitchen.

Jack slowly got to his feet and ambled to the front door. He grabbed his faded denim jacket from a peg and shrugged into it, instinctively seeking to separate himself from the rest of the household. A little fresh air to chase away the ugly impulses.

D. Winston Kent could do with a bit of straightening out. Jack would teach the counselor a thing or two about *closure*. He'd like to start by closing the "new daddy's" eye with his fist.

He would have liked to, but it wouldn't happen, of course. Such a barbaric display would accomplish nothing, except to reinforce his ex-wife's assumptions about his character.

When he stepped outside, the icy, brine-scented wind whipped his hair and billowed his jacket. The rain-swollen sky appeared ready to disgorge its burden any second. It looked like there was a real nor'easter brewing, though the weatherman hadn't said anything about a storm.

He strolled across the sloping lawn to where it gradually gave way to beach grass, scrub pines and beach-plum shrubs. He stood at the top of a log staircase that led down to the beach and watched the wind churn the bay into whitecaps that slapped the wooden pier.

After negotiating the steps, he strolled across the wet sand, making his way to a rocky outcropping that formed a natural jetty at one end of the beach. The waves were too violent for him to climb the jetty and walk out into the bay as he'd done during previous visits. Morosely he realized he might never again have the opportunity. It wasn't likely that he'd be a welcome addition to any holiday get-togethers once Meg and Winston tied the knot.

His presence was barely tolerated now.

The crushing emptiness of his life hadn't eased in the two years since their divorce. If possible, he missed Meg more with each lonely day. He still reached for her every morning before he opened his eyes. And still felt the same heart-clutching sorrow to find her side of the bed empty.

After the initial anguish and accusations, the establishment of support payments and visitation, their infrequent interactions had become polite, efficient. He almost would have preferred a return to the excruciating first weeks. As raw and wounded as he'd felt then, at least their emotions had been out in the open. Strained civility was a killer.

Jack turned and headed back the way he'd come, feeling none of the serenity he'd hoped to find at the shore. If anything, his thoughts were more disordered, his sense of loss deeper, more enervating, than before.

He shouldn't have come. He should have turned down Tanya's invitation.

Waves crashed and receded, licking the beach, leaving the sand smooth and foam flecked and studded with pebbles and small shells. He squatted occasionally to examine the sea-tossed offerings. By the time he reached the steps his hoard consisted of a tiny clamshell, a smooth black stone and a piece of green beach glass, its sharp edges long since blunted by nature's giant tumbler of sand and water.

Treasures for his little girls.

He held the beach glass up to the sky. The meager light barely penetrated it. Probably began life as a bottle of Heineken, tossed from a yacht. This one was for Marie, he thought, she of the runaway imagination. She'd be fascinated by its frosty translucence, by the sense of mutability it represented—only she'd call it "morphing." He smiled, anticipating the tale she was sure to spin, the long and complex history she'd assign this bit of oceanic litter. He dropped the play-pretties into his jacket pocket, where they clinked together musically.

He took the log steps two at a time and started across the lawn toward the house. A movement in the distance drew his attention to the woodpile, covered with a blue plastic tarp. He was just able to make out two figures on the far side of it, locked together in a writhing clinch. He saw the back of a blond head and felt like he'd been kicked in the gut. Meg.

The figures turned slightly and Jack realized he was looking at Tanya's chemically enhanced mane, not his ex-wife's gleaming corn silk. The young man whose tonsils she was attempting to suck out sported a chestnut ponytail; his lean, youthful build was enhanced by designer blue jeans.

Neal Stanton. Pete's twenty-two-year-old son by his first wife, Caroline—the wife who'd stood by Pete through more than twenty years, the wife he'd dumped for young Tanya Willis as soon as the big money started rolling in.

Neal and his father had never been close, but when Pete so callously discarded Neal's mother, their relationship hit rock bottom. Neal had been seventeen then, openly contemptuous of both his father and his new stepmother. Jack didn't think his feelings toward Pete had changed much, but as for Tanya...

Jack couldn't say he was surprised to see these two in a lip lock. He'd suspected it for some time and had to believe that Pete did, too. After all, Neal and Tanya weren't exactly paragons of discretion or restraint.

Jack wondered if this was Neal's way of punishing the old man.

He was thinking it was no more than Pete deserved when the first fat drops of rain pelted him, and he sprinted back to the house.

"WOW, IS IT EVER coming down out there!" Holding the curtain aside, Tanya peered through the rain-lashed window. The panes chattered in their frames, buffeted by the wind.

Meg kept her eyes on the carrots she was cutting. "This is a real nor'easter, all right. Everything closed up and battened down?"

"Neal and Jack are double-checking all that now. I better go change. Unless you need some help...?"

Meg restrained a disgusted sigh. "No, everything's just about done." *No thanks to you.*

"Cool." A little finger-flutter wave and she was gone.

Marie asked, "Can I go play in the rain?"

Meg looked over her shoulder at the backs of her three little girls, lined up in order of size, sitting on bar stools at the opposite counter. They'd spent the better part of the day beautifying one another. Their hair was teased, braided and bound by every pin, barrette, headband and hair tie they could lay their little hands on. Their afternoon of glamour would have culminated in the application of pilfered makeup and nail polish if Meg hadn't caught them in time.

She had put them to work mashing sweet potatoes. It would be a nice plus, she thought, if any potatoes actually ended up in the baking dish. The turkey had another hour or so to go; it smelled divine. When the bird came out of the oven, the rolls would go in.

She said, "Marie, honey, this is a bad storm. You could get hurt if you go outside. The wind would knock you down."

"It's a nowa-ster!" Daisy announced. "Like you, Nowa."

"Is not!" Nora said. "It's called a nor'*easter*."

"Nowa-ster, Nowa-ster..."

"Daisy, stop eating the marshmallows," Meg said. "They're for the sweet potatoes."

"Daddy!" Marie called. "We're helping Mommy make Thanksgiving!"

"I can see that."

Meg looked up to see Jack standing in the doorway. His long legs were crossed at the ankles; one broad, denim-clad shoulder was holding up the doorframe. It was the same indolent pose she'd witnessed countless times before. But now his clothes were damp, his unruly, light brown hair wet from the rain. He obviously hadn't shaved that morning, and the beard stubble delineated every dip and groove in his face...the strong line of his jaw...that dimple in his right cheek as he smiled at her.

She swung her gaze back to the carrots, knowing what his next words would be.

"How are my girls?"

The response was a spirited chorus: "Rich, young and sexy!" He'd trained them well.

He sauntered into the room and lifted the dish

towel Meg had tucked into the front of her apron. As he slowly pulled it out, he stared at her, wordlessly urging her to meet his eyes, but she refused.

At the edge of her vision she saw him take off his jacket and toss it over a chair. He ran the towel over his face, then his hair, and when a damp curl fell over his forehead, it took every ounce of her willpower to keep from reaching up to smooth it back.

He joined his daughters at the counter. "I don't think I've ever seen sweet potatoes done with quite this much enthusiasm," he said.

"Ith got marthmallowth in it!"

"Now, Daisy honey, you know you're not supposed to talk with your mouth full. Here." He sat next to her. "You look like a giant sweet potato. If you're not careful, someone's gonna cook you and eat you up 'cause you're so sweet."

He used the towel to wipe the gooey orange stuff off Daisy's face and hands. He gave her a conspiratorial wink as he swabbed the sticky marshmallow from her mouth, his touch gentle yet confident. He was good at stuff like this.

He was good at all aspects of being a father.

Meg gave herself a mental shake. No, he wasn't. Parenthood meant more than wiping your kid's face. It meant creating a stable, secure environment. It meant putting your family's needs above your own immature, Peter Pan inclinations. It meant settling down and bringing home a regular paycheck—as in the same damn amount every two weeks, every month, every year. Something you could count on.

She and her mother might have started out on the same path, made the same initial mistakes, but at least Meg had had the grit and self-respect to cut her losses before it was too late. Out of the misery of her upbringing she had learned two hard-won lessons—basic truths that had escaped her mother, until it was too late. Meg had learned that passion alone can't sustain a family. And men don't change.

"What did those carrots ever do to you, darling?"

Somehow Winston had sneaked up on her. She looked at the mangled tubers on her cutting board.

"Whatever are you doing to them?" he asked.

"I'm assassinating them. What does it look like I'm doing?"

"Been slaving over a hot stove too long? Getting a little testy?" He chuckled, exchanging a polite nod with Jack.

She leaned on the counter. It was going to be a long four days. "If you really want to know, I'm tired and I burned my hand and I'm all sweaty."

"Mother always says, 'Horses sweat, gentlemen perspire, ladies glow,'" Winston said.

Meg whipped off her apron. "Well, this *lady* is glowing like a pig. I'm going to take a shower."

"Meg!" Winston called, as she swept past him and through the door.

"Best to let her be when she's like that," Jack said. He'd gotten all three girls cleaned up, and had managed to scrape a respectable amount of sweet potato off the counter and into the baking dish. Marie was supervising the placement of marshmallows.

"But I've never seen her so agitated." Winston looked genuinely perplexed. "What did I say?"

"It's not you. It's Meg. She gets a little snippy when she's beat, that's all."

"I have these deep-breathing exercises I do sometimes, to help me cope with my less civilized moods. Perhaps I could teach them to Meg."

Jack bit the inside of his cheek and managed not to smile. "You know, I'll bet she'd appreciate that."

Winston strolled around the kitchen, hands clasped behind his back, inspecting the meal in progress. He smiled his approval at Meg's meticulously constructed yeast rolls. The dough had been rolled into uniform little mounds, two mounds to each well in the muffin tins.

Jack said, "I'll bet you smoke a pipe."

Winston smiled. "You'd lose that bet, my friend. Mother disapproves of tobacco in all forms. It's the smell, you see. It gets into everything."

Mother saddles him with a name like Winston Kent and then forbids him to smoke? "Your mother and Pete will get along famously."

Winston chuckled and shook his head. "Quite the character, Meg's uncle Pete." He glanced furtively at the door and added sotto voce, "Perhaps a bit of a crackpot."

"A rich crackpot." A rich, sadistic, meddling, unscrupulous crackpot.

Winston paused at the sweet-potato station to admire the girls' industry. "What kind of dessert are you making there?"

Marie said, "This isn't dessert, it's for dinner. Sweet potatoes and marshmallows."

"Why, how...novel." He examined their outrageous hairdos. "I see you girls have been having fun with your little hair things." He spoke very slowly, eyebrows raised. "I trust you put everything back just where I showed you? Your little brushes and combs and all your other little accoutrements? Hmm?"

Marie and Nora exchanged a look that told Jack they already had this guy's number. Daisy asked, "What's cootie-monts?"

Winston flicked one of Nora's six braids. "Okay. You've had your fun. Run along upstairs now and make yourselves presentable. You don't want to sit down to Thanksgiving dinner looking like that, do you?"

Marie looked like she'd been slapped. Nora's hand flew to her hair. Daisy tugged on Winston's tweed jacket. "What's cootie-monts!"

Jack slowly got to his feet, expressly to impress Meg's geek-to-be with his height advantage. Recognizing this for the immature, Neanderthal tactic it was, he did a few of those helpful deep-breathing exercises and felt a lot better.

He said, "That's right, girls. I'll bet you brought along some real pretty dresses. Go on up and change into them, and be careful not to muss up your *gorgeous new hairdos* while you're at it. *Right*, Mr. Kent?"

The counselor looked like he was sucking on a lemon. "Yes indeed. Lovely hairstyles. Stunning, really."

The girls ran out, thrilled at the prospect of looking even prettier.

Winston said, "It would seem I have much to learn about—"

"I'm only gonna say this once, so listen up." Jack took a step forward, deliberately encroaching on the counselor's personal space. "Those little girls have only one daddy, and you're looking at him. You want to learn how to be a father, you go make your mistakes on someone else's kids."

"I assure you, my friend—"

"I'm not your friend. And I'm not finished. If you ever do or say anything to hurt one of my daughters, you'll have to answer to me."

He watched indignation and caution battle it out behind the other man's narrowed eyes. Winston folded his arms. "Perhaps Meg was right after all when she asked you to leave. You seem determined to make ours an adversarial relation—" The lights flickered and blinked out, enveloping them in near darkness. "What the devil...?"

From upstairs came a chorus of three piercing, high-pitched screams. Cursing under his breath, Jack sprinted through the living room and took the stairs three at a time. As he loped toward the girls' room, he heard them calling for Meg, who was no doubt still in the shower.

He opened the door, to find his daughters huddled in the middle of the room, stripped down to their Looney Tunes underpants. He crossed to the window and opened the drapes, to let in what little light there was.

Marie screeched, "Daddy, get out! We're not dressed!" She sprinted to a bunk bed and dived under the sheets as her sisters howled with laughter at her newfound modesty.

What a time for his seven-year-old to decide she had something to hide. Feeling foolish, he stood behind the door and said, "The lights went out because of the storm, okay? It's nothing to worry about. Just sit tight. I'll be right back." He rummaged around in the hall closet, located a flashlight and passed it to Nora through a crack in the door. He heard them fighting over it immediately.

Sounds of conversation floated up from the living room—Neal and Tanya speaking in hushed tones. Jack couldn't make out the words.

Meg had taken the room next to the girls. When he'd pressed her, she'd blushingly assured him that Winston never spent the night at her home on Long Island. It would be inappropriate with three impressionable young daughters in the house.

But Jack assumed Winston had his own place. Unless he lived with Mother Kent, of course. An unwelcome image slammed into his mind, of that self-important dweeb in some posh bachelor apartment, furiously humping Meg between starched linen sheets. He probably didn't even sweat.

"Man," Jack mumbled, "don't do this to yourself."

3

WITH THE LIGHTS OUT, the bathroom was pitch-dark, the window shrouded by a heavy shade and curtains. Standing in the old claw-foot tub under a hot shower, Meg groped for the water-control lever and turned it the wrong way. A burst of icy spray squeezed a hoarse scream from her throat.

She screamed again as the shower curtain was suddenly whipped aside and the water abruptly stopped running. A large, powerful hand closed over her mouth while another snaked around her back to haul her up against a long, hard, thoroughly male form.

Warm breath tickled her ear. "Hush, honey, the girls are wired enough without hearing their mama screaming bloody murder."

She pulled his hand off her mouth. "Jack." She was breathless, shivering from cold and a surge of adrenaline. He helped her out of the tub. "The girls...are they okay?"

"They're having a blast. Don't worry about them."

"The door...it's open."

He kicked it closed. Now she didn't even have the gray rectangle of the doorway with which to orient herself. There was only velvet blackness...and Jack.

He pulled her close, enfolding her in his heat, heedless of the water soaking into his clothes from her wet skin. She knew she shouldn't let him do this, shouldn't let him stroke her wet hair and run his big, hot hand down her spine.

But it was dark and her senses were filled with him, with the seductive power of his touch, the heady masculine scent of him, the feel of her breasts crushed against his thin T-shirt, absorbing his warmth and the rhythm of his heart.

"We—we shouldn't—"

"Shh..." He pressed her head to his chest and she allowed herself to relax against him. Just for a few moments, she let herself be seduced by the fantasy that nothing had changed. That she hadn't spent the past two years painfully alone, missing the feel and smell of this man, the low, melodic timbre of his voice in the dark as he whispered of devotion and endless craving.

He dipped his head and she felt his damp hair brushing her cheek, his beard stubble scraping her shoulder. And then the warm satin of his lips on her neck, the barest touch, a whisper of sensation. She shivered anew and his arms tightened around her.

"You smell so good," he murmured. "You always smell so damn good."

He boldly cupped her bottom with one hand and drew her hips into the cradle of his. She felt the power of his need, the insistent ridge against her belly. She moaned, a helpless, desperate sound.

"It'll never be any other way between us, Meg. We'll never stop needing each other." He punctuated his words with a subtle movement of his hips that left her dizzy with longing. Still, she managed to pull back.

"There's more to marriage than that."

He was silent and she wished she could see him, could see the expressive blue eyes so like his daughters'. At last he said, "Was I cruel to you, Meg? Did I abuse you? Did our children go hungry?"

"Not yet."

She heard his sharp, indrawn breath. In a tight voice he said, "The brew pub's doing real well."

"I'm happy for you."

"That's it? 'I'm happy for you'?"

"It's all I can give you, Jack. Don't make this harder than it has to—"

He hauled her to him. Held her fiercely and whispered into her hair, "What happened, Meg? What happened to the life we built together? You and me. Remember what we used to say? That we're a team? That together we can do anything? When did that change?"

She drew in a shaky breath and let it out. "It was an illusion. Hopes and dreams built on vapor. I tried, I tried to make it work, but I just...couldn't take it anymore. The insecurity. It ate away at me. I'd always promised myself I wouldn't fall into that trap."

His fingers tightened on her scalp. "Don't do this, Meg. I'm not your father."

He gently set her away from him. In the blanketing darkness, he asked the question she'd hoped never to hear. "Would you have married me if you hadn't gotten pregnant?"

"Jack, don't—"

"Answer me, dammit!"

She forced the truth past her constricted throat. He deserved that at least. "No. I wouldn't have married you."

Her admission seemed to take on a life of its own, making the air heavier, the room smaller, snapping the last fragile thread of hope.

A knock on the door startled them both. "Meg? Are you in there, darling?" *Winston.*

She cleared her throat. "Yes. I'm here."

"Are you all right?" She heard the doorknob turn.

"No! I mean yes. I'm fine. Don't come in."

His indulgent chuckle carried through the door. She dropped her forehead to Jack's chest and he kissed the top of her head.

"Very well, darling. I'll see you downstairs."

Jack felt around and produced a towel. She let him dry her in the dark. His hands still knew her well. She tried to ignore the buzz of desire his touch engendered, as her body swelled and flowered and wept for a joining that was not to be.

He finished by toweling her hair. When he draped the damp terry cloth over her shoulders, his fingers brushed her nipples, stiff and aching. He was right. It would always be like this between them. She couldn't hope to hide her response. Even in the dark.

He reached for her, as she knew he would. She grasped his wrists and whispered hoarsely, "No. We can't do this."

Slowly he pulled back. After an eternity she sensed

him moving, saw a sliver of gray, partially blocked by his shadow.

"The hall's clear." His voice was composed. Remote. "I'll go check on the girls." And he was gone.

She hadn't lied when she said she'd tried to make it work. At first she'd thought Jack would change on his own, once he was responsible for a wife and child, once he'd become a "family man." Foolish of her. Had she learned nothing from her mother's mistakes?

When he showed no inclination to settle down and get a real job, she found herself turning into what she most despised: the hectoring wife. For all the good it did her. Even the obligations of fatherhood didn't sway him. All she'd accomplished with her nagging was to erect a barrier between them.

With his brains and ambition he could have had a wonderful career, could have completed his degree part-time and gone on to law school, med school. Anything. It would have been rough the first few years, but could it have been worse than what they'd endured?

Or instead of a professional degree, he could have gone to work for some big company. Medical plan, pension, the works. They could have been a normal middle-class family.

It was all she'd ever wanted since she'd been old enough to know such a thing existed. Was that asking too much?

She'd found out too late the answer was yes. Jack had been determined to set up shop, be his own boss, despite the inherent risks. He was convinced he'd never be satisfied working for anyone else. As if the rest of humanity were deliriously happy working nine-to-five for a paycheck!

Every time they argued about it, Meg felt the same sick, gut-clenching fear. The fear she'd come to know too well growing up with a shiftless father and a spineless doormat of a mother.

For the first couple of years Jack worked odd jobs while he learned the microbrewery and pub-management businesses, investigated licensing regulations and made the necessary contacts. Meanwhile Meg clipped supermarket coupons and learned sixty-two ways to serve spaghetti. She offered to get a part-time job, but with two toddlers to care for and another on the way, they both knew that was unrealistic. Somehow they managed to scrape by. As Jack had said, they never went hungry. They always had a roof over their heads.

Just before Daisy was born, he and Kevin Mann located a site, pooled their resources and applied for a small-business loan. The Wolf Mann Brew Pub was a reality.

Getting the pub up and running was more of a challenge than anyone had anticipated. There were problems with equipment, personnel and quality control. Disagreements with Kevin about advertising, cash flow and insurance. Meg's guts twisted into knots every time she thought about the hefty bank loan hanging over their heads. She wondered how long it would take her husband to realize he'd bitten off more than he could chew.

Between the fledgling business and three small children, there was never a moment to relax together, to unwind and talk about their hopes and fears—or to simply hold each other and recall the special bond that had brought them together in the first place. They were too wrapped up in the minutiae clogging their lives, the plodding, day-to-day effort of just getting by.

The arguments escalated. Exhausted from his grinding schedule, Jack came home each night long after the girls had been put to bed. More often than not, he ended up slamming out of their rented apartment and sacking out God knew where. Perhaps at Kevin's or even the pub. Meg never suspected another woman. When would he have found the time?

After a year of this, when her nerves were ready to snap, Pete renewed his offer of employment with his game company. He lured her with the promise not only of a generous salary but flexible hours as well, a valuable perk for a working mother. And, too, Meg knew her sister Laurie, who lived on Long Island, would be happy to keep the girls while she was at work; they'd be with their aunt and cousins, not hired help or a day-care center.

Yet she refused Pete's offer—again—in the misguided assumption that she owed it to her husband to stick by him and support him in his chosen profession, even if it was a pipe dream.

Wasn't that what Mom had always done? Stood by her man?

Daddy's starting a landscaping business, Meggie. This

one'll be it, you'll see. Course, he'll have to borrow a lot of money for a truck and the equipment, but he says he'll make it back the first summer, and then some! He's got it all worked out, honey. We'll move out of this old trailer and get a real house. You'll see.

At least Meg had finally stopped deluding herself. Jack was never going to change. Not for her and not for their daughters. He simply didn't want to.

Uncle Pete was persistent, and the prospect of a generous, regular paycheck became more and more seductive. Still, she resisted until that last big blowup, after some catastrophe struck the brew pub, something to do with mash tuns and tubing. She'd never understood the specifics. As much as Jack had tried to get her interested in the business, she'd purposely avoided learning about it. If she ignored it, maybe it would go away.

During this crisis he left the apartment before she awoke and returned in the wee hours. They didn't see each other for three days. Finally she waited up one night to confront him when he staggered in at two in the morning. As soon as she saw his face, she knew the timing couldn't be worse. He was past exhaustion, on the verge of collapse, his temper close to the surface. But she was frustrated, had bottled up too much for too long.

She said things then. Vicious, wounding things. Things she'd thought but never dared to voice. Things she hadn't even known were inside her, festering, waiting for a moment like this. And he gave as good as he got.

For five years she'd struggled to overlook her husband's nature and the harsh lessons she'd learned at her mother's knee. Tried to fool herself that *her* marriage was different, that Jack had nothing in common with her father.

That night, as she stared into her husband's weary, tormented eyes, she'd known it was over. She felt no relief, only a deep, oppressive sadness.

She'd never stopped loving him. Even now she loved him, wanted him in every way a woman could want a man.

If only that could ever be enough.

"WHAT DO YOU CALL this stuff again?" Pete upended his bottle for a huge swallow. He'd declined a glass.

"It's an amber ale," Jack said.

"Not bad. Hey, Winston, bet you didn't know there's a Murder Won movie script in the works." Pete squirmed in his favorite easy chair, looking decidedly uncomfortable in the dress slacks and wing tips Tanya had no doubt badgered him into wearing. He was a baggy-trousers-belted-below-the-big-gut kinda guy.

"My word," Winston said. He sat on the sofa next to Meg, sipping delicately from a glass of merlot. "A movie based on your board game. Quite a coup, that."

The girls were upstairs in their room playing Barbies, while the adults had congregated in the living room to enjoy a preprandial cocktail by candlelight. The lights were still out, and the storm showed no sign of letting up.

Meg sat stiff and still with her fiancé's arm draped

possessively around her shoulders, clearly ill at ease with her ex looking on.

Good.

Seeing her in the flickering glow of the candles and the fire blazing in the hearth was almost more than Jack could bear, taking him back to candlelit dinners they'd shared as newlyweds. Her skin glowed against her simple, black silk dress; her hair was a river of gold. Her gold-green eyes looked dark and mysterious. God, she was beautiful.

And she was someone else's. Her engagement ring captured what light there was, glowing like a beacon. With every movement of her hand, the thing winked at him. Mocked him.

Jack reached for a chicken canapé. At least it looked like chicken in the meager light. He took a bite and forced himself to chew and swallow. Grilled eggplant, doused in some kind of funky vinegar. He started to set it on his cocktail plate when a slim hand restrained him.

"I'll finish that for you, Jack."

Tanya was perched right next to him on the arm of the sofa, so close he could count the diamonds on her ankle bracelet. To give thanks for God's bounty and to honor her Pilgrim forefathers, she'd selected a screaming-hooker red slip dress that barely covered her breasts, thighs and giblets.

She raised the tidbit to her mouth and made a private show of savoring what had passed from his lips to hers. Well, not quite private. Even in the dim light Jack saw Meg's jaw tighten, while Neal sat slumped in

a deep leather club chair, nursing a tumbler of bourbon on the rocks and glaring sullenly at Jack.

Tanya lifted the bottle of merlot. "Winston?"

"Oh, no, thank you, Tanya. I never have more than
one glass."

Jack imagined Mother Kent's invisible hand patting
her boy on the head.

"We're getting a Saturday morning Murder Won
cartoon show off the ground, too," Pete announced.

"Kinda rough for kids, no?" Jack asked. Feeling his
hostess sliding closer still, her breath hot on his neck,
he leaned forward, as if eagerly awaiting Pete's answer.

"They're tying it in to a new version of the game
coming out next year—Murder Won Junior."

"Good Lord."

"You got a problem with that, Wolf?"

"Do I have a problem with hawking a game to impressionable kids that glorifies murder?" He could
sense Meg holding her breath, and experienced a per-
verse pleasure in taking his time selecting another
hors d'oeuvre—endive with smoked salmon; safe—
and eating it slowly while the tension in the room
swelled to a quivering crescendo.

He grinned. "Hey, who could have a problem with
that, right? You're the new director of marketing,
Meg. You don't have a problem with it, do you? Hell,
maybe you could test-market it with our own kids,
whaddaya think?"

He knew that look of hers. Too still. Too controlled.
As if her face might crack at any moment.

What the hell was he doing?

Going out with a bang, not a whimper, perhaps.

Pete had a funny little smile on his face, as if he'd just picked up a second pair of kings. Jack felt the hairs on his nape rise up and salute that smile.

Pete said, "So what you're saying is, maybe some kid'll play my game and maybe it'll influence him to do something rotten. Something maybe even illegal. Like knocking over a liquor store, maybe. Is that what you're saying?" He took a long swig of his amber ale, keeping Jack in his sights.

Jack sat very still. He felt sweat start to bead on his upper lip.

"You didn't answer. Is that what you're saying, Wolf?"

The room was unnaturally quiet, except for the roaring in his ears. Everyone was waiting for his answer.

It wasn't possible. Those records were closed. Jack smiled. *He's bluffing. Bastard has an instinct about these things. It's what makes him such an animal in business, but it's only a guess. He's got nothing.*

"Yeah," Jack said. "I guess that's what I'm saying."

Pete's eyebrows rose in mock admiration. "Noble sentiments, Wolf. Thing about noble sentiments, though, they have this funny way of coming back and biting you on the ass."

He held Jack's gaze a long, sickening moment—*he's got me!*—and showed his hand. "I wouldn't go spouting all that holier-than-thou crap if *I'd* done fifteen months in Sing Sing."

Meg's gasp cracked the air like a bullwhip.

Reading Jack's mind, Pete added, "It's amazing what a good PI can sniff out."

Tanya became unnaturally subdued at her husband's mention of a PI.

"What were you in for again?" Pete asked. "Oh yeah, armed robbery. A liquor store, am I right?"

"You enjoying yourself, you son of a bitch?" Jack barely heard his own low, rage-choked voice.

"Jack...?"

He looked at Meg, leaning forward, her face white, her eyes wide and stricken.

"Jack, what's he talking about?"

He glanced around, noted Neal's mean little smirk, Tanya's take-me-now body language. "I won't discuss it here."

"What's he talking about, Jack?" Meg tried to rise, and Winston restrained her with a hand on her shoulder and a gentle word in her ear. Bastard must be enjoying this almost as much as Pete.

Jack rose. "Come with me, Meg. I'll explain—"

Winston said, "Don't go anywhere with him," and something inside Jack broke free of its leash. He lunged for the counselor, seized his collar in both fists and slammed him hard against the sofa before he even knew he was moving. Neal and Pete sprang to their feet.

Jack said, "You don't tell my wife what to do." It was a ragged whisper, strangely disembodied. He stared at his own hands mangling Winston's jacket collar, and slowly unclenched them. Meg's fiancé glared at him with such cold hatred Jack had to look twice. He hadn't thought the man capable of real fire or passion.

Maybe he did sweat in bed.

Jack had to do something with the raw fury that was eating him from the inside, before he lost control altogether. Mechanically he stalked three paces to the wall adjoining the den, hauled back and slammed his fist through the Sheetrock. Chunks of plasterboard rained onto the hardwood floor.

Pete sneered, "You're not so high and goddamn mighty now, are you, Wolf?"

Why had he never realized how truly evil Meg's uncle was? Fleetingly Jack wondered how long Pete had known about his past. Why bring it up now?

The answer came in the next heartbeat. Hadn't he felt Pete's malignant gaze whenever he and his ex-wife had been together, even when they'd been amicable?

Especially when they'd been amicable.

Perhaps Pete had feared a reconciliation was in the works and decided to nip it in the bud. If so, he'd done a first-rate job.

Meg rose shakily to her feet. When Jack moved toward her, she said, "No. I'm not going anywhere with you. I'm not interested in what you have to say."

"Meg—"

"The fact is, I just don't care. Your life ceased to concern me when I left you."

"Meg, for God's sake, honey, I was a kid. Let me—"

"Give it up, Wolf," Pete said. "She dumped you

even before she knew you had a record. What makes you think she wants to listen to your crap now?"

Jack stared him down. "You did everything in your power to break up my marriage. But even that wasn't enough, was it? Get one thing straight." He took a menacing step toward Pete. Neal and Winston reacted with a little jerk, like puppets on a string.

Jack could not tell himself later that he spoke in haste, without thinking. The truth was he'd never been so clearheaded. "If you interfere with my family again, I will kill you."

The ugly threat hung in the air, dense and menacing, like gasoline fumes waiting for a random spark to set them off.

"I'm hungwy. Can we eat now?"

All eyes swiveled to the dark hallway over their heads. Jack could just make out Daisy standing there, clutching her cowgirl Barbie. His heart kicked so hard it nearly threw him off balance. How much had she heard?

Meg managed to answer, "Y-yes, honey, I think we're ready." Marie and Nora appeared then, and the three girls pounded gleefully down the stairs and into the dining room.

Jack had no intention of sitting down to dinner with Pete, until Meg threw him a beseeching look: *Pretend everything's normal. For the girls' sake.*

If he'd ever seen her looking more miserable, he couldn't remember. He'd always done this to her, he thought. Brought her heartache when all he'd ever wanted was to make her happy.

He'd pretend everything was normal if it killed him.

"MMM...WHO MADE THIS yummy sweet-potato casserole?" Jack made himself scoop up a large helping of the orange glop with its crust of browned marshmallow. His stomach was being squeezed by a giant fist; forcing anything into it would be an effort.

Daisy rose to the bait. "*I* did!"

"You only ate the marshmallows!" Marie charged.

Nora said, "Daddy, you're wearing the shirt we gave you for your birthday."

"That's right, sweetie. It's my favorite shirt."

"And you're not scratchy anymore," Marie said.

He ran a hand over his smooth jaw. "You didn't like my whiskers?"

She wrinkled her nose.

"*I* liked them," Tanya said. "They made you look rugged. Like some...I don't know...*lumberjack.*"

Pete and Neal speared Jack with identical baleful expressions. They'd never looked more alike.

Nora said, "Please pass the stuffing."

Jack was about to praise the politeness of her request when Winston intercepted the serving bowl. "You may have more stuffing when you finish your green beans, Nora."

Nora whined, "The beans are gooey!"

Marie said, "Eat the crunchy onion stuff on top. That part's okay."

Jack sent a wordless message to Winston, who defiantly held his stare for one long, sizzling beat. Winston was the first to break eye contact, muttering, "I don't suppose it would hurt to skip your green vegetables just this once."

Meg's alert gaze ricocheted from her fiancé to her ex-husband. That look said, *Did I miss something here?*

Neal turned to Tanya. "After dinner I wanna show you that sugar bowl of Great-grandma Fleming's I told you about."

Who did Neal think he was fooling? Jack wondered. Did the little weasel actually believe no one had noticed the two of them slinking into the house through separate doors earlier? Soaked to the skin? With wood chips clinging to their clothes?

Neal and Tanya had put their heads together, ostensibly to discuss Great-grandma Fleming's crockery, when Pete announced, "The old broad's sugar dish'll have to wait. We're all gonna play Murder Won after dinner."

Neal pried himself away from his stepmother to say, "Tanya and I will take a rain check."

"I said *everyone's* playing. A little murder and mayhem is good for the digestion. Even for a mama's boy like you. You telling me there's no one at this table you wouldn't like to bump off?"

The flesh around Neal's eyes tightened fractionally. His gaze slid away from his father, and a mottled flush crawled up his throat. Tanya patted his arm and whispered something in his ear.

Oblivious, Winston said, "Well, I for one would love to try my hand at this game of yours, Pete. Reminds me of Thanksgivings when I was a boy. We always gathered in the music room after dinner for some cutthroat backgammon."

Pete said, "You want cutthroat, you're in for a treat. This is no fairy-mary backgammon. It's life or death. Kill or be killed. Survival of the fittest."

Neal picked up his fork. "Hey, Jack. I thought you ex-cons had your own special eating style. You know." He hunched over his food in demonstration, his arms circling his plate, his eyes sliding around the table suspiciously.

Pete snickered. Winston appeared to be biting back a smirk.

Meg's stricken eyes met Jack's. Just for an instant. Long enough to make him wonder if she was humiliated for him—or for herself, for having ever been Mrs. Jack Wolf.

Daisy asked, "What's a ex-con?"

Jack laid his fork on his plate. "You know, Neal, teaching you some manners would almost be worth the trip back to Sing Sing."

"Jack..." Meg's tortured whisper sliced right through him.

Daisy cried, "I wanna go to Sing Sing!" What a jolly-sounding place.

Pete said, "That brother of yours...Mike, is it?"

Meg groaned, "Pete, please..."

"He still there? At Sing Sing?"

Jack watched Marie and Nora exchange wide-eyed stares. They'd never been told they had an uncle. "It's Mitch," he said tightly. "And yeah, as far as I know, he's still there." Pumping iron and filing appeals.

Not even for Meg would he subject himself to this. Rising with as much dignity as he could muster, he politely excused himself and went in search of something stronger than amber ale.

4

"...TWO, three, four, five. Strychnine! Yes!"

Meg watched Winston gleefully slam his playing token on the space on the Murder Won game board corresponding to Jack's Weapon card. Jack—or more accurately, his game character, Jack the Ripper—was Winston's assigned victim in this round. Winston's character was Ma Barker, his plastic-and-cardboard token embellished with her likeness.

The point of the game was survival. The last one left alive was the winner. Every player was not only an aspiring murderer, but a victim as well, the target of another player's lethal intent.

Players could move their tokens in any direction along the meandering, intersecting paths of the board. To murder your victim, you had to land on the three Weapon, Motive and Location spaces that matched the three cards your victim drew at the beginning of the game. But you could acquire the corresponding card only if you correctly answered a trivia question related to a historic murder.

If you managed to collect all three cards, your victim was officially iced—and out of the game. In that case you inherited not only your victim's assets, but his or her intended victim as well, giving you a fresh target to pursue.

A howling gust of wind rattled the windows. Far from abating, the storm seemed to be getting worse. The pounding of wind and rain was a constant backdrop. Pete had announced that he had a gas-powered generator in the toolshed, some distance from the house. No one had volunteered to brave the elements to fetch it. Tomorrow would be soon enough. The phones were down, but Pete had brought his cellular phone to the island, so they weren't cut off from the outside world.

Winston turned to Jack. "Your days are numbered, my friend."

"Not if you keep on the way you're going, *my friend*. You've landed on that space three times and you haven't answered a question right yet."

"I have a good feeling about this time," Winston said. He turned to Meg, keeper of the Interrogation cards. "Shoot."

Neal obligingly aimed a finger at Winston and mimed a trigger pull. He still had that tumbler of bourbon in front of him, Meg noticed. He'd refilled it a couple of times.

She'd known Jack had no intention of joining them for a rousing game of Murder Won, not after...everything. But she'd asked him to, as a personal favor. They had the next three days to get through, and if the tension level didn't ease, they'd all be basket cases by Sunday.

He'd studied her expression searchingly. Pete's

dreadful revelation stood between them like a glass wall. Blandly she'd returned his stare, and at last he'd slid his gaze away, with a weary little smile. *Sure, Meg*, he'd said. *If it's what you want, I'll play.* She knew he'd relented in part simply to spend more time with her.

She drew the top Interrogation card and held it near a candle. "Who killed Lucrezia Borgia's husband?"

"I know that one," Neal said.

"Shush!" Winston waved him to silence. "That's a giveaway. Old Lucrezia herself did the deed."

Meg had never seen her fiancé so animated. Still, she was forced to give him the bad news. "Wrong. Lucrezia's brother Cesare killed him."

Neal said, "Who?"

"Give me that!" Winston snatched the card from her fingers, glanced at it and tossed it back.

Pete unwrapped a cigar and clipped the end. "Told you this was no game for sissies, Ma. Better luck next time."

Jack tossed the dice and moved his Jack the Ripper token, groaning when he overshot the Motive space he was aiming for: *Life Insurance Windfall.* He'd already collected Pete's Weapon and Location cards— *Garrote* and *Taj Mahal*—by landing on those spaces and answering the questions correctly.

Meg watched Jack shake a few more sunflower seeds onto the table. Was he chagrined or secretly pleased to have drawn her uncle as his murder victim tonight? His placid expression offered no clue. He never once glanced at Pete, whose token bore the likeness of John Wilkes Booth.

He did look at Meg, though, his crystal eyes smoky in the candlelight. Not furtive peeks when he thought she wasn't looking, but the bold, interested stare she associated with those early months of dating before she'd let him make love to her. Rainy afternoons in the student-union coffee shop, him looking at her that way over cups of fragrant jasmine tea, her body humming with an acute, almost painful awareness of his nearness, his heat, his knee brushing hers under the table. The artless sensuality of his long fingers as he idly twirled a coffee stirrer.

If there was anything untoward in Jack's regard now, none of the other players seemed to notice. She told herself she was hypersensitive, emotionally ravaged by the events of the day.

Tanya rolled the dice and moved her Lizzie Borden token eleven spaces, where she was instructed to pay twenty-five thousand dollars in blackmail money. She flung a raw oath and began counting out hot pink Payola chips. Legal fees were paid with neon green Shyster chips, and guns and other weaponry with blaze orange Ammo chips.

She cursed again. "Seventeen grand. That's it. I'm flat busted."

Meg couldn't help herself. Despite her efforts to ignore Jack, she caught his eye and almost lost it. If there was one thing Tanya *wasn't*...

"Story of that gal's life," Pete said, grinning around his reeking cigar. "Never has enough cash."

Neal tsked. "You know what happens to naughty little ax murderesses who don't cough up their hush money." He snatched Tanya's Lizzie token and held it over the open top of the little plastic cage attached to the playing board. "No no!" he squawked in a high-pitched voice. "Not *Death Row!*" He dropped Lizzie into the cage and strapped her into the tiny electric chair.

"Goodness," Winston said. "I guess it's curtains for Lizzie."

Pete said, "And you thought backgammon was cut-throat."

Meg had accepted her promotion to marketing VP before the decision was made to create a kids' version of Murder Won. Jack's words had hit home, mirroring her own misgivings. Did she have the stomach to institute an aggressive campaign for this malevolent game aimed at children her daughters' age?

Pete had developed Murder Won seven years earlier, when he still owned the handful of service stations he'd inherited from his father. He'd always loved mystery games, but those already on the market were too tame for him, so he invented his own. A few inquiries with the major game companies resulted in two offers, both of which he rejected. He sold the service stations and started his own business in Queens, New York, producing and marketing Murder Won.

It was a gamble that paid off. Faced with the near impossibility of getting his product into stores under an independent label, Pete started with mail-order sales. Word of mouth spread and soon Murder Won became the hot item to own, more popular than Trivial Pursuit in its heyday.

If anything, the unpolished sales brochure and the obscurity of Stanton Game Company, Inc., intrigued jaded murder-mystery fans and boosted sales. Within a year Murder Won was flying off store shelves as well. The game and its various spinoffs had made Pete Stanton millions.

Meg could only marvel that this quirky game that began life seven years ago with a small underground following was now poised to invade Saturday morning kiddie shows.

After Tanya succumbed to Old Sparky, it was Meg's turn. She tossed the dice and moved her Al Capone token, landing on a Location card she had no use for: *Oval Office.* The game progressed as, one by one, players were annihilated.

Eventually Jack and Neal were the only players left. Neal had only one of the three cards necessary to kill Jack, the *Ice Pick,* while Jack held two of Neal's cards: *Fired Unjustly* and *Alamo.*

Jack hurled a steady stream of taunts at his opponent while patiently attempting to land on the space corresponding to the last card he needed, *Rusty Scythe.* He kept throwing the dice and overshooting.

While Neal grew increasingly agitated, Jack appeared serene, almost bored. Lazily munching his sunflower seeds, he exuded an air of sublime confidence, even when Neal captured his Motive card, called simply *Lust.*

At one point Jack smiled at Meg, that lazy, knowing grin that always made her wonder if he could read her mind. Only then did she realize she'd been nervously twisting a strand of hair. She dropped her hands to her lap.

At last Jack landed on *Rusty Scythe*. A funny grinding sound came from Neal's throat. Jack looked at Meg, awaiting the question.

She drew an Interrogation card and read: "Who assassinated Archduke Francis Ferdinand and his wife, Sophie, in 1914, thus precipitating the outbreak of World War One?" She laid down the card and folded her hands, biting back a knowing smile of her own.

Pete chuckled and sucked on his cigar. Neal leaned back in his chair, allowing himself a little smile of triumph.

Jack frowned. Scrubbed at his jaw. Blinked in perplexity. Neal snickered and reached for the dice, but Jack stayed his hand.

"This is just a shot in the dark, mind you, but, well, could it have been that pesky Serb Gavrilo Princip?"

Meg beamed. "Right you are, Jack."

The counselor's eyebrows shot up. "My word!"

Neal's nostrils flared. He held out his hand and Meg dropped the card in it for his inspection.

Tanya said, "Well. You're just full of surprises, aren't you, Jack?"

Jack said, "I was working toward my BA at Binghamton before Meg got...before we quit school to get married."

"Let me guess," Winston said, regarding Jack with something that could almost be called respect. "Your major was history."

"With an emphasis on modern Europe. I never

imagined old Gavrilo would come in handy someday."

Meg was pleased to have Winston's assumptions about Jack thrown back in his face. She knew her fiancé viewed her ex-husband as a lowbrow drudge, and the insulting stereotype rankled. Irreconcilable differences notwithstanding, she'd always respected Jack's intellect and industry, and the fact that he wasn't afraid of hard work. If he'd been willing to direct those qualities into a secure career, they'd still be together.

Or would they? The scene in the living room came back to her with sickening force. The horrific secret her husband had kept from her.

He hadn't even *tried* to deny it. He could have just looked her in the eye and said, "Pete's lying, Meg. He's trying to cause trouble. You know it can't be true."

Instead he'd threatened her uncle's life—a calm, simply worded promise of retribution. Seeing the look on Jack's face, the scary intensity, she'd almost believed him capable of following through.

When that hellishly strained dinner had finally been over, the girls had practically fallen asleep in their pumpkin pie. Together, Meg and Jack carried them upstairs and put them to bed. For a few charmed minutes she allowed herself to pretend that they were a normal family, doing normal-family things.

Together they sang the requisite lullaby, "Hush, Little Baby." Jack had begun that particular bedtime ritual when Marie was a newborn, and he'd serenaded all three girls to sleep with the same song. In the last year of their marriage he'd rarely made it home by the girls' bedtime, but whenever he did, he was the vocalist of choice.

When he and Meg had separated, she'd tried to sidestep the painful reminder of her ex-husband by substituting another song from her limited repertoire, but the girls would have none of it. Only "Daddy's song" would do. So she'd carried on the tradition in her own wobbly soprano for the last two years.

Hearing Jack's deep, velvety voice crooning the familiar words again caused a bittersweet ache to swell her throat. She feigned a little cough, not trusting her voice.

They took turns kissing the girls and making them into "sausages," tucking the covers tightly down the length of their little bodies as they giggled and tried to lie perfectly still. When the two of them stood to leave, Jack laid his heavy, warm hand on her shoulder, just as he often had when they were married. It was a wordless communication, a reaffirmation of love and solidarity—and pride in their daughters, their little miracles. And just as she'd often done back then, she'd reached up to entwine her fingers with his.

And abruptly dropped her hand without touching him....

Pete's gusty sigh jerked her back to the present. Rising, he dropped his cigar stub into his half-filled coffee cup, earning a sneer of disgust from his wife. "Well, folks, as the tomcat said while making love to a skunk,

'I've enjoyed about as much of this as I can stand.' I'm hitting the hay."

SOMETHING WAS TEASING Jack's exhausted brain back to consciousness, something more than the noise of the storm. And much more pleasant. A soft, rhythmic stroking on his bare neck and shoulders.

He sighed and stirred restlessly. The uneven terrain of leather upholstery under the thin sheet he lay on brought him closer to wakefulness, as did a smooth, solid something against his nose that he dimly identified as the back of the sofa.

More feather strokes as the top sheet inched down and he felt cool air on his bare torso.

"Meg..." he mumbled, shifting onto his back. Some primitive part of him sensed the ardent feminine softness hovering nearby. His arms reached for her, his mouth seeking hers, even as a tiny spark of lucidity registered that something was off-kilter.

Greedy hands yanked at his tangled sheet and blanket. "I've waited so long for this."

Tanya! His eyes sprang open, though he could make out nothing in the ink black living room.

He tried to sit up, only to find himself snagged by the covers she was furiously trying to free. She whispered, "Do you have any idea how hard it was, waiting for that old fool upstairs to fall asleep?"

"Tanya—" He grunted as her elbow found his solar plexus. "This is no good."

"Oh, it'll be good." Success. The sheet and blanket went flying. "Take my word for it. It'll be good." She pounced on him like a Doberman on prime rib. She was wearing something silky, and not much of it. Her hair felt wiry against his face. He'd bet it had more chemicals poured into it than a toxic waste dump.

He pushed on her shoulders. "Now, listen, Tanya. This isn't gonna happen. I don't want to hurt your feelings, but—"

"The stubble's coming back." Her nails scraped his cheek. "Good."

He wore only pajama bottoms. When he felt her yank the drawstring at his waist, he seized her hands and bolted upright.

And squeezed his eyes shut against the beam of light that suddenly speared them. "What the hell...?"

Neal's hoarse stage whisper came from the upstairs railing overlooking the living room. "I knew it. You son of a bitch!"

Tanya cursed under her breath. "Here we go."

As Neal raced down the stairs, his flashlight played over the scene of impending debauchery. Jack hurriedly retied his drawstring. "Listen, it's not how it looks."

Neal snorted. Jack would laugh, too, in his place.

Tanya hissed, "You don't own me, Neal. I didn't make any promises." The light found her face and she squinted at her lover defiantly.

Jack braced himself for vitriol, only to hear a whimpering "Jeez, Tanya, how'd you let him talk you into this? I thought we had something special, you and me. I thought you...cared."

She pursed her lips in annoyance. The harsh light

highlighted every little line around her mouth and eyes. Where did this woman come off claiming to be twenty-nine?

Jack ran his fingers through his disheveled hair. "Listen, you guys have a lot to talk about, so—" The light seared his eyes, and he shielded them with a hand.

"How could you do it with *him*, Tanya? An *ex-con*. A *criminal!*"

"You wanna know the truth, that turns me on," she said, chin high.

"Is that what I have to do to keep you?" The light danced maniacally as Neal slammed the flashlight into the back of the sofa. "Knock over a liquor store? Maybe a couple of gas stations?"

She rolled her eyes. "Oh, grow up, Neal."

"Could you guys try to keep your voices down?" Jack pleaded.

"'Cause I'd do it, Tanya," Neal whined. "I'd do that and anything else you asked of me. Anything. You know that. We talked about—"

"We talked about a lot of things," she snapped. "Talk's cheap. And boring. Jack doesn't talk, he takes action. You don't get it, do you, Neal?"

She stood up, hands on hips, and Jack got to see what she was wearing—and what she wasn't. The part that was there was pale green and filmy.

She said, "Jack's not like you. He doesn't snivel and beg and let some woman tell him when something needs doing. He just takes care of business. He—"

"That's enough." Jack stood up, grabbed his sheet

and blanket from the floor and flung them on the sofa. He'd already forfeited one night's sleep driving down from Ithaca. He was running on empty. All he wanted was to get some shut-eye. To spend as much of this miserable weekend as possible unconscious. "Get that light outta my face. *Now!*"

He sensed the sudden surge in Tanya's libido, a hot wave of pheromones at this display of bad-boy machismo. The beam of light slowly dropped.

Jack remembered when Neal had been a pimply, snot-nosed kid. It wasn't that long ago. "For what it's worth, I didn't invite the lady here. This was all her idea."

"Shut up!" Neal barked. "You—you just shut up. And you!" The light swung from Tanya toward the hallway that led to the den. "Come with me, woman. Now!"

She muttered, "Oh brother," and threw Jack an eloquent look. He knew she wasn't looking forward to spending the next hour or so pretending to be helplessly turned on by her young lover's exhibition of macho churlishness.

Apparently emboldened by his woman's slavering obedience, Neal paused and directed the beam of light to Jack once more. "And if you want to leave this island in one piece—"

"Don't press your luck, kid."

The light wavered, swung away. He watched their shadows disappear, heard Tanya's whispered words, placating Neal.

Jack flopped back onto the sofa and pulled the sheet up. Could the weekend get any worse?

JOHN WILKES BOOTH CHEWED *on his stogie and snarled, "How about that look on your wife's face when I told her you're a lousy ex-con!"*

Jack the Ripper threw down his sunflower seeds and pulled out a long knife. "I'll kill you, you meddling son of a bitch!"

Jack lunged for Booth and stabbed him in the heart, again and again. The blade made a dull thudding noise that grew louder and louder....

Meg jerked awake. The bedroom was nearly pitch-black. Rain hammered the windows. Tree branches scratched at the glass like bony fingers.

She rolled onto her stomach and pulled the pillow over her head, hoping to blot out some of the noise. And praying she wouldn't dream about a showdown between Ma Barker and Lizzie Borden.

When she awoke again she was still lying on her stomach with her arms circling her head. She rolled over and found she had no feeling in her right arm. With her left hand she lifted it like a lump of clay and rested it on her middle. She lay there a few moments feeling the rush of blood shoot sparks into her fingertips. She flexed her hand, swung her legs over the side of the bed and sat up.

It was still dark. She groped for the matches and candle on the nightstand. By the flame's meager light she peered at her wristwatch: 2:54. The storm hadn't let up at all. Would the girls be able to sleep through it?

She rose, not bothering to cover her flannel nightgown with a robe, and carried her candle out into the hallway. She peered over the railing. Jack was down there, she knew, sleeping on the sofa, but the flickering halo of candlelight didn't reach that far.

She inched open the girls' door and tiptoed inside. This room was furnished with two bunk beds. Marie slept smack up against the safety rail on one of the top bunks, her leg dangling over the side, the flashlight clutched to her chest.

The other top bunk was mussed but empty. Checking the bottom bunk, Meg found Nora and Daisy curled up together, their limbs flopped over one another. She could only assume Daisy had awakened, disoriented by the strange surroundings, and Nora had abandoned her own bed to comfort her little sister. Meg smiled and dislodged the tangled blanket enough to cover them.

She left quietly and turned back toward her own room, only to stop short. Something niggled at the corners of her awareness, something…out of place. She peered into the gloom, struggling to discern detail.

Then she saw it. At the other end of the horseshoe-shaped hallway, directly across the chasm of the two-story living room. The door to the attic, half-open. It had been closed when she'd gone to bed, she was certain.

With the candle held before her, she made her way around the horseshoe. Her steps slowed as she approached the attic door, held open by an object, some sort of bundle lying on the stairs and spilling into the hallway.

Laundry, she told herself. Even as her heart pummeled her rib cage.

Laundry. Even when she saw. Even when she crouched down and held the candle over it.

And then she was scrambling backward, the candle slipping from her numb fingers as a scream raced up her throat, a long, low, wounded-animal sound that never made it past the hand she clamped over her mouth.

The candle sputtered and winked out and there was only darkness. And the dead thing on the attic stairs.

5

MEG NEVER KNEW how she made it to the top of the stairs, only that she found herself there on her hands and knees, groping in the dark, muttering a string of nonsensical oaths under her breath. And with only one thought in her head.

Jack.

She had to get to Jack. Jack would know what to do. He'd hold her and ground her and make the horror go away.

Her icy fingers encountered the smooth wood of a newel post and she pulled herself up, leaning on the banister lest her quaking legs give out. She inched down the stairway in the pitch blackness, her ragged breathing sounding like a freight train in her ears. She oriented herself with the help of the faint glow of coals in the hearth. She couldn't see the sofa, but she knew where it was in relation to the fireplace.

Blindly she stumbled across the room, knocking into an end table and righting a lamp in the nick of time. She fumbled around and found the sofa's leather upholstery.

"Jack!"

Her mouth formed the word, but no sound emerged. Or perhaps the slamming of her pulse simply drowned it out. She felt her way to the front of the sofa and sank to her knees, relieved beyond measure when her trembling hands located his warm, sheet-draped back, when her nostrils filled with the familiar, comforting scent of him.

"Jack...Jack..." she whispered, shaking his shoulder. "Jack, wake up!"

He groaned and rolled over, his deep voice raspy with sleep. "Tanya...good God, woman, you're insatiable!"

Meg jerked as if scalded. Suddenly her mind was clear—too clear—all panic and dread forgotten. She slapped his shoulder hard, the resounding *thwack!* loud as a gunshot. In the same instant, she gained her feet. "*Get up!*" she demanded.

He bolted to a sitting position, his voice incredulous. "Meg?"

"So sorry to disappoint you," she hissed.

After an instant's hesitation he muttered, "Damn..."

"I should've known! You and that floozy!"

"Meg—"

"I just thought you had more taste! How could you?"

"Meg, calm down. I didn't—"

"Save it!" she snapped. "I don't care, remember? I don't care what you do with your life. It doesn't concern me anymore."

"Yeah," he said dryly, "I can tell."

She sensed movement and realized he was rubbing his shoulder where she'd whacked him. Shame crowded out all else for a moment. Neither of them had ever raised a hand to the other in anger, not even during the worst of their arguments. What had come over her?

"I—I'm sorry," she said. "I shouldn't have...I didn't think, I just..."

"Forget it. What's wrong?"

It struck her with sickening force what was wrong. She looked helplessly toward the doorway to the attic, though she could make out nothing in the gloom.

"Meg?"

Shakily she sat next to him on the sofa. "Something's ha... There's been a..." She squeezed her eyes closed and concentrated on making her mouth work. "We have an emergency."

She felt him stiffen, felt him turn toward her. "One of the kids?"

"No. Not the girls. They're fine. It's...Pete. He's..." She forced the words out. "He's dead."

Jack was utterly still for a long moment. When he spoke, his voice was quiet and even. "What was it? His heart?"

"I don't know. It—it might've been."

"Has Tanya called the police yet?"

"Tanya? I haven't seen Tanya. I came right here."

Only then did she realize she'd run to Jack, and not Winston, in her moment of need. The idea of seeking out her fiancé had never occurred to her.

Habit, she told herself. It meant nothing.

Jack said, "I just assumed she woke you up. Pete's not in his bed, then?"

"No. He's in the hallway, at the bottom of the attic stairs. I found him."

"Oh, honey." His warm hand settled on her shoulder and gave it a squeeze. "I'm sorry. That must've been rough." He rose and fumbled for something on the end table. "You stay here."

"No. I'm coming with you."

He lit a candle. "It's not nec—"

"I don't want to be alone."

The admission escaped before she could restrain it. In the wavering candlelight she read gentle compassion in his eyes, and she relaxed. He'd always been able to do that—offer his strength and support without making her feel weak for needing it. She swallowed a knot of unwelcome emotion.

He raised a hand and trailed his knuckles down her cheek, never taking his eyes from hers. "It's all right," he whispered. "I'll take care of it. The worst is over."

She exhaled sharply, tears of relief burning her eyes. During the past two years she'd forgotten how much she'd once relied on this man, in big and little ways. He was steady, levelheaded. He could take any crisis and turn it around, make it right.

This wasn't the kind of crisis that could be made right, of course—no one could perform that particular miracle—but she knew in her gut that Jack would take charge of this horror and absorb the worst of it.

He took her hand and led her back to the stairway. Their surroundings took on an otherworldly feel as they silently climbed the steps and made their way down the hallway, Jack leading with his candle.

He stopped near the open attic door, shielding her from the sight with his body. She saw everything vividly anyway, in her mind's eye. Uncle Pete lying on the attic steps, his head and shoulders spilling into the hall, his neck twisted at an unnatural angle. His eyes just barely open.

Jack knelt and set the candleholder on the carpet. He placed his fingers on Pete's fleshy throat, going through the motions of feeling for a pulse, something she hadn't had the presence of mind to do. She didn't imagine he expected to find one. He slowly took his hand away and shook his head.

Pete wore a voluminous Chinese silk robe over his black satin pajamas, belted below his huge gut. The robe was emerald green, richly embroidered, with a thick stuffing of silk between the quilted layers. He'd had it custom-made in Hong Kong the year before, and had bragged to Meg about the great bargain he'd struck. He'd brought her back a string of cultured pearls from the same trip.

"Pete..." She pressed a hand to her mouth and tears spilled over it.

And then Jack was there, pulling her into his arms, pressing her face against his bare chest. He held her tightly while she sobbed out her shock and sorrow. Pete had been no angel. He was crude and belligerent more often than not, but he was family. Her mother's half brother.

"We can't leave him here," she rasped, lifting her head from Jack's chest. "The kids'll be up in a couple of hours."

"The police might not be here by then. I don't think you're supposed to move a body, but under the circumstances, I don't see that we have a choice."

His gaze took in her uncle's lifeless form, before swinging up the darkened attic steps. His expression gave away nothing, but she knew this man too well, could almost hear the gears turning in his head. Examining the possibilities.

She shivered. "He—he must've had a heart attack or something and fallen...." Jack didn't respond. "Right?"

"Did you notice the head wound?"

She felt her throat start to close up. "No," she croaked. Jack had examined Pete more carefully than she had.

"Well, it's...bad. I suppose it could've happened in the fall."

"You *suppose?*"

"I mean it must've."

She suspected he didn't mean any such thing. She glanced at her uncle's still form once more and turned away, took a deep breath. "We ought to wake up Tanya. She's got the cell phone. We should call—" She stopped abruptly. And turned slowly to look once more. Her heart kicked into high gear.

"What?" Jack was watching her closely. "Meg, what is it?"

"His ring." She made herself approach the body. She looked closely at Pete's right hand, lying on his broad middle. The fingers were bare, as were those on his other hand, thrown up over his head. The extravagant diamond ring was nowhere to be seen.

Jack murmured, "That's strange. Pete's worn that thing for years."

"Five years. It was his gift to himself when Murder Won brought in its first million. He's never taken it off, Jack. Never. He told me he sleeps with it on, showers with it on. It's some kind of good-luck thing with him."

Their gazes locked. She didn't like what she read in his eyes.

He said, "What was he doing up there in the first place? In the middle of the night?"

She shook her head, at a loss.

"What's going on?"

They turned to see Tanya standing a short distance down the hall, near the doorway to the master bedroom she'd shared with her husband. In the flickering candlelight she looked like Marilyn Monroe's ghost, her voluptuous curves enhanced by a filmy belted robe that hugged her generous breasts and swirled around her ankles in a froth of pale green silk.

Meg fought the mental picture that bubbled up from some corrupt corner of her imagination. Tanya and Jack, writhing on the living room sofa in sheer animal lust. Jack touching her, kissing her, driving himself into her.

The knowledge that her ex-husband had chosen to share himself with this shallow, selfish woman was too painful to contemplate. Somehow it tainted all that Meg herself had shared with him, the purity and beauty of the act that had sealed their love and conceived their children.

Meg forcibly squelched her own irrational jealousy—petty in the extreme, considering the grief in store for Pete's wife. Tanya's view of her husband was obscured by the dark, and by Jack and Meg, who closed ranks for that very purpose. Meg found herself shaking, anticipating the other woman's reaction. She didn't like or respect Tanya, but no one deserved this kind of shock.

Jack said, "Tanya, there's been an accident."

Tanya frowned. "What do you mean?" Her eyes widened. "Where's Pete? He's not in bed."

Meg approached her. Her impulse was to take her hands, but her own were so cold and clammy, she didn't dare. "Pete went up to the attic. We don't know why. He...he fell down the stairs, Tanya. I'm sorry." Her voice caught, and she felt the reassuring weight of Jack's hand on her shoulder.

He said gently, "He's dead. I'm so sorry, Tanya."

She appeared stunned, taking it in. Then she abruptly shoved between the two of them and stared at her husband's body.

Before her scream could approach the higher decibels, Jack slammed a hand over her mouth and pulled her back against him, murmuring, "Okay, I know, I know, but we've gotta keep it down, Tanya. The kids..."

Tanya turned in his arms and buried her head in his bare shoulder, clinging to him like a barnacle. She sobbed prettily. Too prettily. Meg instantly berated herself for the catty observation. *Give the woman a break*, she told herself. *Think what she must be going through.*

Meg was thankful the girls' room was the farthest from this spot, their heavy oak door firmly shut, and that they were sound sleepers. She knew from experience that you could launch a mortar in their room without disturbing their slumber.

After a minute Jack peeled Tanya off himself. She pressed the back of her hand to her mouth. "Not Pete. Oh my God, not my Pete," she wailed, and launched herself at Jack once more.

He offered Meg a sheepish glance over the platinum head, which he gave a few soothing pats before once more setting Tanya away. Firmly.

He said, "We need to call the authorities. Where's your cell phone?"

Tanya pressed a hand to her heaving chest. "In my room. On the dresser."

Meg said, "Take her down to the kitchen, Jack. I'll bring the phone."

"No, you take her. I'll get the phone," he quickly said, backing away before she could contradict him. "I'll meet you down there."

Meg detoured to her room, Tanya in tow, to grab her robe and slippers. In the kitchen she found a dozen candles and lit them all, hoping the light would chase away the destructive emotions that had wormed their way into her consciousness. The niggling doubts and suspicions. Not to mention that old green-eyed monster.

Outside, the storm had abated. A light rain pattered on the window glass.

Tanya stood before the reflective door of the microwave, wiping smeared mascara from under her eyes and finger-combing her hair. She adjusted the plunging neckline of her robe before turning to Meg. With a shuddering sigh, she said, "This is all just so unreal. What will I do without my Pete?"

Meg knew better than to tackle that one. "I'll make coffee." Thank goodness for the huge propane tank outside that fed the gas stove.

Jack entered the kitchen a minute later, the small gray cellular phone in his hand. He'd thrown on jeans and a black T-shirt, but he was still barefoot, his wavy hair disheveled. "Tanya, do you have another battery for this?"

"Battery?"

Meg paused in the act of scooping coffee and closed her eyes, praying she'd misheard him.

"The battery in this phone is dead." Jack's voice was too calm, each word too carefully enunciated, a dangerous tone Meg knew well.

Tanya said, "Oh. Yeah. I called a few friends. It stopped working after a while and made that funny beeping sound."

A muscle in Jack's cheek jumped. "You used the cell phone *after* the house lines went out? For nonessential calls?"

She propped a hand on her hip, slack jawed. "Well, duh! What was I supposed to do—use smoke signals?"

"Do. You. Have. A. Backup."

"A backup?"

Meg quickly interjected, "A second battery."

"No."

Jack took a deep breath. "Did you bring the charger for it? We could recharge it off the portable generator."

"Uh, no." Tanya's expression revealed she was beginning to get it.

Jack just stared at her for long moments, then met Meg's eyes. She still held the full coffee scoop poised over the percolator basket. "No phone," he said with deceptive calm, and tossed the worthless thing on the counter.

Oh God. She dumped the coffee grounds in the basket and mechanically counted scoops, trying to find solace in the routine task.

Tanya flounced to the table and sat. "Well, it's not my fault."

Meg leashed her tongue, her sympathy for this silly woman wearing thin.

Jack said, "Did Pete have a two-way radio?"

Meg answered. "Only on his yacht."

"Which is at some boatyard, right?"

"In Freeport." She sighed, adjusting the flame under the percolator and leaning heavily on the counter. "It's being refurbished over the winter."

He said, "I don't suppose the *counselor* has a cell phone."

His acid tone brought Meg's head up. She stared him down, her expression carefully neutral in front of

Tanya, but he got the message. After a few moments his jaw worked and he glanced away.

"No," she said. "He wanted to relax this weekend—didn't want anyone at the firm to be able to reach him."

Tanya's face lit up. "Wait a minute! We're not cut off!"

Jack and Meg turned to her expectantly.

"Neal has a laptop computer," she smugly announced. "He can send E-mail to the police."

"Tanya, all the lines are down," Meg said.

Tanya rolled her eyes. "It's a *laptop*. It has a *battery!*"

"You need a phone line for a modem," Meg explained, her patience near the breaking point. At Tanya's blank look she added, "The modem allows you to connect the computer to the phone, which is how you E-mail people."

Tanya's chin went up. "I knew that."

Jack said, "I'm going to go wake up Neal and Winston. We have to get Pete moved before the kids get up."

Meg suspected he was equally eager to escape Tanya's presence before he could say something he'd regret. One thing she'd always admired about Jack was his ability to keep a rein on his temper. Now that she knew the truth about his past, she couldn't help but wonder if that was a survival skill he'd learned in prison.

Prison. The thought of her ex-husband behind bars was, as Tanya would put it, unreal. The fact that he'd never told her about it was just as shocking. Would it have made a difference? Would she have fallen in love with him anyway? She couldn't say. All she knew for sure was that it had been unforgivable of him to withhold this from her, whatever his reasons.

The comforting aroma of coffee began to permeate the room as the brew finished perking. Meg carried a mug to Tanya and had started to pour one for herself when an outraged bellow from upstairs made her start. She yelped as scalding coffee sloshed over her knuckles. Slamming the percolator back on the stove, she charged out of the kitchen toward the stairs, stubbing her toe on the newel post in the dark.

The kids' ability to sleep through anything was being put to the test this night.

A flashlight beam bounced around near the attic doorway. She made out the forms of the three men as she raced up the stairs.

Holding the flashlight like a weapon, Neal advanced on Jack, who stood his ground. "Did you think you'd get away with this?" He shook off Winston's attempt to restrain him. "You killed my father, you son of a—"

"Neal!" Meg said. "Calm down. You know that can't be true."

He turned toward her, and in the eerie half-light he looked wild-eyed and dangerous, the picture of stark rage. She'd never seen him like this, and it frightened her.

He growled, "He killed him so he could have Tanya—the rich widow. Did you know about them, Meg? Did you know the two of them have been—"

"That's enough!" Jack said.

While Meg knew that Neal spoke the truth, she wondered how he had the nerve to revile Jack for what he himself had done. No one bothered to point out that with his father gone, Neal had just as good a shot at snagging the "rich widow."

Which got Meg thinking about Tanya herself. With her husband dead, she was a...well, a rich widow. With at least two virile young lovers eager to console her.

Neal glared at Jack. "Why'd you swipe the ring? Force of habit?"

Winston said, "This is neither the time nor the place for such accusations. Jack's right. We must move Pete before the children awaken. Neal," he added gently, "the two of us can handle this. You needn't be involved."

Meg was impressed by her fiancé's compassion and his levelheaded response to this crisis.

Neal said, "Forget it. I don't trust him. Let's just do it."

Winston glanced at his companions. "Where?"

Jack said, "The boathouse. It's dry and it's far from the house."

"And, too, the temperature has dropped," Winston observed delicately. "Is that all right with you, Neal?"

"Whatever." The young man's malevolent gaze was still on Jack. Did he really believe Jack had killed his father? Meg decided to give him the benefit of the doubt and assume his words were the result of shock,

and the lingering effects of all that bourbon he'd guz-
zled.

Returning his attention to the task at hand, Neal
scratched his head and said, "How are we going to get
him out there? I think there's a tarp in the toolshed."

Jack and Winston exchanged a look, clearly reaching some silent accord. Winston said, "Meg, why
don't you go down and keep Tanya company? I don't
think she should be alone right now."

Jack must have seen her reluctance to spend another
minute alone with the widow Stanton. He added, "Go
on, Meg. Keep her in the kitchen. We'll let you know
when we're finished here."

She opened her mouth to object, but something in
their solemn expressions stopped her cold.

Oblivious, Neal studied Pete's body from a different angle. "I think there's a wheeled dolly out there,
too. If one of us gets above him on the stairs—"

"Neal," Winston interrupted. He sent a silent message that seemed to get through. Neal glanced at Meg
and snapped his mouth shut.

Now they were all staring at her. She had the sudden and uncomfortable sensation that she didn't belong here. They saw this as a male chore, she realized,
this nasty business of transporting hefty, recently deceased uncles who'd managed to get themselves
wedged into awkward spaces. The womenfolk were
to be spared the unpleasant details.

For once, this liberated woman was more than
happy that chivalry wasn't quite as dead as poor Un-

cle Pete. "Right," she murmured, backing toward the
steps. "I'll, uh, go see how Tanya's doing."

She hurried down to the kitchen.

IT TOOK THE MEN longer than Meg had anticipated to
move Pete's body to the boathouse. Or perhaps it only
seemed to take forever, sequestered as she was with
the widow. Every sound from beyond the door—
grunts and low murmurings, the occasional heavy
thud—jangled her nerves.

Stuck in the kitchen with only Tanya's self-absorbed
chatter for a diversion, Meg turned to the stove for dis-
traction. She made a double batch of her special corn
muffins, though she couldn't imagine putting anything in her stomach except coffee.

Just before 5:00 a.m. the electricity came back on.
Meg raced to the wall phone, only to find it still dead.
"Damn!" She slammed it back on its cradle.

For her part, Tanya had occupied herself with the
latest issue of *Cosmopolitan* until power was restored,
at which point she began channel surfing on the small,
under-the-cabinet television set and complaining
about the absence of cable stations on the island.

"There's, like, nothing on at this hour!" she said for
the umpteenth time, switching from the yoga show
back to a rerun of *Ben Casey*. "I don't think I've ever
been up this early."

Jack finally came in to give the all-clear, looking
damp and bedraggled and heartbreakingly bleak.

For one insane moment Meg had the urge to go to
him—to hold him, soothe him, kiss away the lines of

strain on his face. Instead she remained rooted to the spot and said, "Is everything okay?"

"As okay as can be expected."

"I made corn muffins." She toyed with her hair. "My special recipe."

The faint smile that just reached his eyes told her he hadn't forgotten his favorite breakfast. She chose not to dwell on the silly impulse that had prompted her to bake corn muffins this morning.

"They smell good," he said, but she could tell he was just being polite. She didn't imagine his appetite was any keener than hers just then. "I'll eat later. Right now I just want a shower, followed by about a gallon of hot coffee."

"I'll put another pot on."

Jack turned to Tanya. "How are you holding up?"

Tanya sighed heavily and looked away, her chin trembling.

Meg had spent the last hour and a half cooped up with this woman, who'd displayed not a hint of grief until Jack stepped through the door. She had to resist the urge to roll her eyes at the theatrics. If that made her cold and cynical, so be it. Her compassion had reached its breaking point.

And if Tanya expected Jack to pull her into his arms and comfort her, she was in for a disappointment. Keeping his distance, he mumbled some worn-out platitude and disappeared through the doorway.

Meg made her escape shortly afterward, ostensibly to check on the girls. They were still sound asleep, God bless them. She stood at the entrance to her room, staring at the door to the attic, now closed. Jack was still in the shower; she could hear the water running. Winston and Neal were in the kitchen with Tanya. The sounds of conversation drifted up to her.

Without letting herself think about it, she made her way along the hallway to the very end. The only clue that anything was amiss was the bare hardwood floor. The hallway was carpeted in Oriental runners, a separate carpet for each of the three segments of the horseshoe. The piece along this stretch had been removed, bringing to mind the head wound Jack had mentioned. There must have been blood.

She rubbed her tired eyes and wondered how they were supposed to get through the next couple of days without a phone.

She whispered, "What were you doing up there, Uncle Pete?" Practically of its own volition, her hand turned the doorknob. The door swung open and she flipped the light switch, illuminating the bare wooden staircase leading to the attic.

Lifting the hem of her robe, she climbed the steps and entered the dusty, unheated room. She pulled the robe closer around her to ward off the chill. Two bare bulbs hung from the rafters. The small window at the end of the room had an eastern exposure, revealing a drizzly sky struggling to go from black to gray.

Old furniture was stored here, along with original artwork amassed by four generations of residents. Meg lifted a sheet and ran her hand over a beautiful rolltop desk of bird's-eye maple, still in perfect condition after a century and a half. This piece had occupied a corner of the master bedroom until Pete had married Tanya five years ago. Then it and most of the other antiques had been relegated to the attic to make way for the modern furnishings she selected. Tanya couldn't see the point in keeping "all this old stuff" around.

Cartons of assorted household items, books, toys, photographs and sports equipment were stacked along one wall. Anything left by a vacationing relative or friend eventually had found its way up here.

Meg lifted the flap on a cardboard box and immediately spied the old Frisbee Pete had given her when she was eight. It was a "tournament" model, its edges marked by innumerable nicks and gouges, thanks to the Stantons' old collie, Bozo, who'd long ago gone to doggie heaven. Her family's infrequent holidays with her uncle and his first wife had been the highlights of Meg's childhood, a rare break from the misery and want of her youth.

Smiling gently, she closed the box and glanced around. The smile faded when she recalled what had brought her up here. Answers. What was Uncle Pete doing in the attic in the middle of the night?

She walked the perimeter of the room, past sheet-draped dining chairs and a motley assortment of tennis rackets that probably dated to the previous century. The steel door of a wall safe peeked out between two stacks of cartons set against a knee wall. This safe had fascinated her as a child. Her imagination had conjured up a pirate's hoard of treasure filling the thing to overflowing—jewels and gold coins and stacks of hundred-dollar bills.

As far as little Meg had been concerned, anything was possible. This vacation home, after all, belonged to the "rich relatives." And that was *before* Pete made millions from Murder Won. Almost anyone had been rich compared to Meg's family.

She tugged on the safe door experimentally, just as she'd always done as a child. As then, it was locked. She wondered if the key still existed, whether this safe was even used anymore.

She continued her excursion around the room—and stopped cold when she spotted an object lying on the floor near the top of the stairs.

A baseball bat. An old wooden one, decades old by the looks of it. She squatted and stared at it, afraid to touch it, afraid of where her imagination was leading her.

"Get a grip, Meg," she admonished herself, and lifted the thing to study it. She turned it in her hands, examined the hitting surface, knowing what she was looking for and hating herself for it. Aside from grime worked deep into the grain, it was clean.

If a bat like this was used as a weapon, would evidence remain? Blood? Hair? What if the surface had been wiped down afterward? If there had been fingerprints, she'd compromised the evidence by handling it herself.

She set the bat down. How could she even be thinking this way? It was all Jack's fault; his careless words lingered in the back of her mind, nagging her.

Did you notice the head wound? I suppose it could have happened in the fall....

She started to rise and was arrested halfway by something else that caught her eye, a tiny object wedged just under the edge of a carton of photograph albums.

She plucked the black-and-white sunflower seed from under the box and examined it in her palm. Her eyes cut from it to the baseball bat. She curled her fingers around the seed and fought the memory that shoved its way into her mind. Jack confronting Uncle Pete.

You did everything in your power to break up my marriage.

She squeezed her eyes shut, trying to force the ugly scene from her consciousness.

If you interfere with my family again, I will kill you.

I will kill you.

Everyone had heard him say it.

She uncurled her fingers and stared at the seed. The question she kept asking resurfaced once more, but she was no longer directing it to her dead uncle, she was directing it at Jack.

"What were you doing up here?"

6

JACK RAISED THE AX and brought it down in one smooth movement.

Crack!

The impact rippled through his arms and shoulders. He raised the ax again, along with the piece of wood it was now buried in, and slammed it down on the tree stump. The wood split, and the two pieces clattered to the ground. He bent to retrieve them, then added them to the woodpile.

This was what he needed, he thought. Mindless physical labor. Just the thing to focus his energy and get his mind off the bizarre horror show this family gathering had become.

He and Meg had broken the news to the girls together, in a gentle, straightforward manner. They'd explained, in terms the children could understand, that Uncle Pete had had a heart attack, though privately, Jack had his doubts about that.

Sweet, sensitive Nora had wept, seeking solace in her mother's arms. Little Daisy had popped her thumb in her mouth and patted her sister's back soothingly. Marie had asked if Uncle Pete was in heaven. Knowing what his own answer would have been, Jack had let Meg handle that one.

Though the temperature had dipped into the low forties, he'd managed to work up a sweat and had discarded his denim jacket. He wiped his face with the tail of the old gray S.U.N.Y. Binghamton sweatshirt he couldn't bear to part with, though it was worn and faded and ragged at the shoulders where he'd hacked off the sleeves. He had a hard time getting rid of anything that reminded him of his brief college days, that giddy period of discovery and new love...with Meg.

He straightened his back and raised his eyes toward the house. And cursed.

"I've come to give you a hand with that, my friend!" Winston hollered, waving as he strolled across the lawn. He was the epitome of the well-heeled outdoorsman in glaringly new Timberland boots, corduroy slacks and a plaid wool jacket over a pine green turtleneck. A hunter's cap with earflaps completed the rugged ensemble.

Jack's fingers tightened around the handle of the ax. He muttered, "Just what I need—Eddie Bauer, Esquire."

Winston stopped in front of him and took in Jack's progress. "You should have told me we needed to replenish the firewood. I'd have come out sooner."

"There's plenty of wood in the house. These logs aren't even seasoned." He set another one on the stump. "Just something to do."

Whack!

Winston said, "I suppose it's difficult for someone of your inclinations to remain idle for long."

Jack looked at him. "My inclinations?"

"Your predisposition for manual labor. You know." Winston flexed his arms. "Earning one's bread by the sweat of one's brow. Good honest toil. The backbone of our economy."

What a condescending jerk. Could this guy hear himself? What did he think Jack did for a living, lay railroad track? *Get on back to the house and your adoring fiancée.*

"I don't need any help," Jack said.

"Nonsense." With a glance at Jack's bare, sweat-sheened arms, Winston stripped off his jacket and cap, and tossed them on the woodpile, though his breath was smoking. "So." He rubbed his palms together. "Is there another ax?"

"Nope." With the counselor looking on, shivering visibly now, Jack split two more logs.

He detected an unspoken agenda behind Winston's offer of help, something that went beyond mere boredom or the desire to lose himself in hard work. Jack hadn't exactly seen sparks flying between Winston and Meg—although that might have been his own wishful thinking. He knew Meg had always admired his own easy physicality. He was pretty sure it turned her on.

And the counselor knew it. Jack could have laughed—it was suddenly all so clear. This Daniel Boone display was for Meg's benefit. Winston would show her he was every inch the manly man her ex-husband was. Well, far be it from Jack to stand in the way of this touching courtship display.

"On second thought, why don't you have a go at

it?" He handed over the ax to a beaming Winston and watched him select a log.

"I must admit, you're a tad more experienced at this than I." Putting his back into it, Winston sheared a thin chunk off the side of the log, losing control of the ax in the process. It skidded off the stump and pierced the ground an inch from his foot.

Jack leaped back a step. "Uh, that puppy's sharp, Winston." He'd just put a fine edge on it with a whetstone.

"My word." An embarrassed flush colored Winston's face.

Taking pity, Jack showed him how to hold the ax, how to swing and how much pressure to exert. After a couple of tries, Winston began to get the hang of it.

He pushed up the sleeves of his sweater. The guy might be middle-aged, Jack admitted, but he was far from flabby. His snug turtleneck revealed a trim, athletic torso.

Jack asked, "What do you do to stay in shape?"

Winston gave a final whack to a log. It separated neatly and he replaced one piece on the stump to split it. "Tennis, downhill skiing, and of course, golf."

"Of course." *Plus fooling around with my wife—don't forget that.*

"Do you golf, my friend?"

"Never tried it. Meg and I went downhill skiing once, but it seemed like a lot of waiting around for the lift and not all that much actual skiing. Plus it made me nuts, clunking around in those damn boots. Cross-country's okay. Mainly I'm into mountain biking, and there's this local baseball league I play with. Winters, I do some boxing at a gym."

"Well, that's great. The important thing is to stay active. It's the key to health and longevity."

Jack restrained himself from adding that taking up with a woman young enough to be your daughter didn't hurt, either.

He hated the strained bonhomie he and Winston were struggling to maintain. Yesterday evening he'd practically strangled this guy in an instinctive, primitive display more suited to cell block D than a holiday get-together. But like it or not, this man was going to be his children's stepfather. Jack was going to have to learn to get along with him. For everyone's sake. *May as well start now.*

"Listen," he said. "I was way out of line yesterday. I had no call shoving you around like that. For what it's worth, it's not my usual style."

"It's forgotten."

Jack looked at him, surprised by the counselor's obvious sincerity.

Winston smiled grimly. "Emotions were running high all around. If I'd stopped to think, I wouldn't have interfered the way I did. Though I don't believe any of us were stopping to think at the time."

Except Pete, Jack thought. Pete had planned out that little scene for the greatest possible destructive potential. Poker-faced, hoarding his little secret like a royal flush, just waiting to spring it on Jack—and Meg.

Winston added, "No one can say you weren't provoked. It's not my way to speak ill of the dead, but in this case..." Idly he planted the ax blade into the end grain of a log and twisted it out again. "I'd venture to say no one will truly mourn Pete Stanton's passing."

"That's a safe bet."

Winston met his eyes, his own serious. "I do care for Meg. I want you to know I'll be good to her and—" He stopped abruptly, obviously wary of stepping on Jack's toes again.

"And to the girls," Jack finished for him. "It's all right. I know what you mean. I guess I'm a little...proprietary where my kids are concerned."

"You have a right. I admit I'm a little clumsy at this extended stepfamily business."

Jack sighed. "Join the club. I guess we'll get the hang of it sooner or later."

Yesterday he'd had the counselor comfortably pigeonholed as a snooty, supercilious, patronizing jerk—an assessment that had left Jack feeling smug and even slightly heartened. He couldn't imagine Meg committing the rest of her life to someone like that.

Apparently neither could she. Belatedly he realized Winston Kent was more than a walking joke in a Brooks Brothers sport coat. The man had depth, maybe even character. Which didn't mean he wasn't snooty and supercilious and patronizing, only that those traits weren't the sum total of his personality. Jack still didn't like him, but he was beginning to see why Meg did.

He found that train of thought less than cheering.

"Lemme have that." He took the ax from Winston and hefted the fattest log onto the stump. For the dozenth time he wished he were home in his empty apartment in Ithaca—or better yet, holed up at the pub, brewing that new raspberry ale he wanted to try.

Winston watched him work for a minute. "May I ask you something personal, Jack? If it's none of my business, just say so."

Jack sank the ax into the log. "Ask me and I'll let you know." The ax came free with a squeak.

"Why did you keep your…checkered past from Meg?"

Another ax stroke. Jack yanked the blade out of the log. "Why do you think?"

"I imagine…I imagine you were afraid of losing her."

"Bingo." The log finally split and Jack centered one of the halves on the stump. "I'll be the first to admit I made some mistakes. Stupid mistakes."

Winston said, "I myself feel honesty is crucial to the success of a relationship."

Jack stopped to wipe his face on his shirt. A wicked idea began to take shape. He felt the devil inside him strain at its leash. "Well, see, that was my one big mistake, Winston, what you might call my fatal flaw. My lack of honesty. That's what broke us up, me and Meg." Even as he thought about his plan, his conscience rebelled. He couldn't do this, not even to Winston.

"I was under the impression your marriage failed because of your disinclination to settle down in a meaningful career and provide a stable income," Winston said, brow furrowed.

Yeah, I can do this. Jack unhooked the devil's leash and set it loose. "Oh, that was part of it, sure," he said. "I don't know what Meg has told you, but that stability business was just the tip of the iceberg. The real problem was that she demands total honesty—I mean *total*—and I guess I always fell short."

"You lied to her?"

"It wasn't so much lying as sins of omission, if you know what I mean." Jack kept his eyes on the wood he was splitting, keeping a straight face.

"No, I don't believe I do."

"Well, Meg always wants to know what's really on your mind. 'Constructive criticism,' she calls it. I can't believe she hasn't told you. It's the damnedest thing! She *demands* to have all her faults pointed out—every little imperfection. And forget about insincere flattery. She can spot that a mile off."

"I never got the impression she was like that," Winston said.

"Oh, she doesn't come right out and say it. And I guess that's what tripped me up. If I'd just known what she expected at the outset, maybe we'd still be together." Jack shook his head ruefully, scrubbing a hand over his mouth to stifle a grin.

Winston still wasn't convinced. "If she's so intent on this constructive criticism, why doesn't *she* criticize *me*?"

"For what?"

He appeared to ponder that. "Well, I really couldn't say."

Jack threw up his hands. "Well, there you go."

"So. She wants total honesty," Winston mused.

"Total. She sees anything less as, well..." Jack turned away, presumably too overcome by shame to face his companion. "As unmanly. To her, a *real man* doesn't hold anything back, no matter how petty or even cruel it may sound. Of course, she'll act all affronted when you do it, but that's just an act. You want to know what I think?" He glanced around, as if to ensure their privacy, and said sotto voce, "I think it turns her on."

Winston's eyes widened and Jack nodded meaningfully.

"My word. What kinds of faults does she want pointed out?"

"Well, let's see...she thinks she has fat thighs."

"*Meg?*"

Jack shrugged. "Women. She wants constant reminders to exercise more and work off the saddlebags. Oh, and those moods she gets in once a month? You know what I mean...."

"Oh. Yes." They shared a masculine chuckle over that.

Jack said, "Well, when she's all hormonal, mopey and depressed, she wants you to snap her out of it. You've gotta tell her you just won't tolerate the whining and self-pity. And don't forget to get on her case about all that hair twisting she does."

He pursed his lips. "Yes, that is mildly annoying."

"And that's just the kind of thing she wants to hear, to help her break the habit. Only don't say 'mildly.'"

"And, too, there's the matter of her language," Winston said.

"Her language?"

"Well, I'm sure you know Meg occasionally uses words that have no place in a lady's vocabulary. I've managed to overlook it, but I'll have to say something to her before she meets Mother."

"Why wait? The sooner you deal with it, the more she'll respect you."

Winston nodded briskly. "I'll speak to her right away."

Jack slapped him on the back. "All I can say is don't make the same mistake I did. My friend."

"I'M A CAT!" Daisy cried, pulling her lather-covered hair into twin spikes on the crown of her head.

"What should I be?" Meg asked, working the shampoo into a froth on her own head. A delicious scent enveloped her—wildflowers and almonds, if the label on the shampoo bottle was to be believed. She and her three-year-old shared the big old claw-footed tub in the spacious bathroom.

"Be a dog. No! Be a dwagon!"

"A dragon! What kind of ears does a dragon have?"

"Big scawy ones."

"I think I'll need some help with that."

Meg bent her head and allowed Daisy to shape her sudsy hair into two long globs that flopped over her ears.

Meg said, "Is my hair too long for this?"

"Nooo...it's just wight! You're a scawy dwagon."

"Should I breathe some fire?"

Daisy giggled. "Yeah! Bweave fire!"

Meg took a gigantic breath, her eyes bulging ominously, and made a production of blowing "fire" at her bath-mate. Daisy squealed in delight and splashed at the monster.

"Shall I save you from the dragon, Daisy?" a voice from the doorway asked.

Meg whipped her head around to see Jack closing the door behind him. For an instant she had the ridiculous urge to fold her arms over her breasts. "What are you doing here?"

His grin was unrepentant as he ambled toward the tub. "Saving my daughter from a fire-breathing dragon, of course. I'm the white knight, remember? Your hero."

She remembered. Something flashed between them before she averted her face, something that squeezed her heart painfully.

"I knocked," he added, "but I guess you didn't hear me over all that splashing and fire breathing."

"I scared the dwagon away," Daisy announced. "Like this." She slapped the water vigorously.

"Oh, so you're the hero. Or heroine, I should say." He squatted by the tub. "You put out the dragon's fire."

"As you can see, we have everything under control," Meg said tightly. "You can leave now."

"Nonsense. I'll help rinse you off." His grin said he was confident she wouldn't make a scene in front of Daisy. The worm.

Suds were sliding down Daisy's forehead, and she started to blink and rub her eyes. He caught her hand.

"Careful, sweetheart. This isn't baby shampoo. It'll sting your eyes." He swiped the lather off her forehead and reached up to slide the showerhead out of its bracket. It was the convertible hand-held kind connected to a hose. He tipped his daughter's head back and carefully rinsed the shampoo out of her hair, shielding her face from the spray with his big hand.

He told her to stand and gave her chubby little body one last quick rinse, then lifted her out of the tub. As Meg watched Jack wrap their youngest child in a thick white towel, she wondered fleetingly what her next baby would look like. Winston had never been married and wanted at least one child. That was fine with Meg, who'd always loved being a mother. But she couldn't imagine bearing a child who didn't have Jack's curly hair, or his expressive blue eyes.

He rubbed Daisy briskly with the towel, blotted her hair and ran a wide-toothed comb through it. "There you go," he said, "one squeaky-clean dragon slayer. Marie's in your room. She'll help you get dressed."

Clutching the big towel around her, Daisy scooted through the doorway and down the hall, giggling. "Mawie! There's a dwagon in the tub!"

Only then did it occur to Meg that he'd done this on purpose—engineered a way to be alone with her, something she'd actively avoided all morning and most of the afternoon, and had hoped to avoid for the duration of this hellish holiday weekend.

He closed the door. She heard the lock click.

She sat up straighter and reached for the shower-head before he could commandeer it. "Goodbye, Jack."

He slid his hands into the pockets of his jeans and walked casually to the tub. He was wearing that old, sleeveless Binghamton sweatshirt that should have gone in the trash bin years ago. He looked pumped; the muscles in his arms were standing out in sharp relief. She recalled then that when she'd last seen him, he was heading outside to chop wood.

He said, "Why so nervous? I don't bite." He squatted by the tub again and casually dragged his finger-tips through the water. "Want me to hotten this up for you?"

She didn't respond, knowing full well that his preferred method of "hottening up" her bath had nothing to do with adding warm water. She turned on the faucet and adjusted the spray, then tipped her head back and rinsed her own hair, thank you very much.

Belatedly she realized her arched position afforded her ex-husband quite an eyeful. She held the shower-head with one hand and finger-combed her wet hair with the other to get all the suds out. If she'd had a third hand, she'd have clapped it over his eyes.

"Stop staring at me," she demanded.

"You've got to be kidding." He smiled the kind of smile he never would have bestowed in Daisy's presence.

"You have no shame."

"Just figured that out, did you?"

She directed the spray at his face. Laughing, he

turned off the water, rendering her weapon useless. He pulled his soggy shirt off over his head and shook his wet hair in her face.

"I mean it!" she said. "What if Winston finds you in here?"

"You expecting him?" He tossed the shirt in a corner.

"Maybe."

She was a lousy liar. And he knew it. "You think there's room in this big old tub for the three of us?" He reached for his belt buckle.

She grabbed his hand. "Don't you dare!"

He relented and picked up the bar of soap instead, wetting it and rolling it in his hands. His chest was wider, his stomach harder, his shoulders broader than she remembered. Under the dark hair that fanned out from the middle of his chest, his skin had a residual summer tan.

He said, "Remember when we used to take baths together?"

She didn't want to remember. "I've already washed."

"You can never be too clean."

He replaced the soap in its dish and glided his hands over her stiff back. The stark pleasure of his touch sent her resolve into a tailspin. He was kneeling now, his warm breath wafting over her, mingling with the fragrant, steamy air. Gradually she felt herself relaxing.

"We used to wash each other, remember?" He moved to the arm nearest him, soaping and stroking it with those long, strong fingers. "I'd do your back and you'd do mine. And we'd move on from there, inch by inch, until I was hard as a post, and you were—"

"Don't," she pleaded, remembering all too well the baths and showers they had shared. They had teased each other far past the point of simple foreplay, until the need was almost painful, a deep, grasping hunger that pulsed like a heart, there where she needed him most. It had been a game, a mutual challenge to see which one of them would beg for it first.

He'd had enormous control. Despite her determination, she would almost always break down first, clutching him, opening to him, shamelessly pleading. Anything to feel him inside her. And he would smile that wicked smile and, more often than not, torment her for another few excruciating minutes before giving her what she needed.

"You do remember," he murmured, reaching for her other arm.

She closed her eyes, shielding her thoughts, knowing he could read her all too well.

She let her arm go limp. He lifted it, caressing it with his soap-slick hands, working the lather along her fingers and between them, before lowering her arm to the water.

He said, "Some things, it's hard to forget." When she didn't respond, he went on the attack and asked, "How about you and the counselor? You ever get dirty while you're getting clean?"

Her eyes snapped open. "You have no right to ask that."

"You're right. Answer it anyway."

As if she'd give him the satisfaction!

Unfortunately, she didn't need to. One look at her face triggered a smile of pure male arrogance.

"I didn't think so." He soaped his hands once more. "At least there's one thing you've done only with me."

He started to wash her breasts, as casually as you please. She seized his wrists, sitting up straighter. "Jack..." He ignored her protest, gliding his hands slowly over her skin, following her contours.

She felt drugged by his touch, making it difficult to remember why she shouldn't let him do this. He gently twisted free of her hold and set her arms at her sides. She left them there.

"Lean back," he said, and exerted mild pressure until she was lying against the slope of the tub, submerged to just above her waist. He rinsed his hands and rolled a towel to cushion her head, then lifted her arms to rest on the sides of the tub. Her engagement ring clicked on the porcelain, a less-than-subtle reminder.

Oh yeah. That's why I shouldn't do this.

"Let me pamper you," he said.

"Is that what you're doing?" she asked dryly.

He met her eyes directly, with the hint of a smile, an expression at once candid and mysterious. Her pulse jumped and she stifled a whimper of longing.

Two years.

Too damn long.

She shouldn't permit this. She mustn't permit this.

She was an engaged woman. Jack no longer had a claim on her.

But he wasn't acting as if he had a claim on her. He was beguiling her, seducing her. And heaven help her, she was allowing it.

He picked up the soap again, and she let her eyes drift shut. One minute. Maybe two. Then she'd stop him.

Her breath caught when she felt his slippery fingers sliding up the sides of her breasts and closing over them, carefully molding the soft flesh. Her mouth parted and her breathing grew shallow. She fought the urge to sigh, to arch into his touch.

He stroked her chest and shoulders, her sides and her sensitive armpits, always returning to her breasts. Her nipples were pinpoints of pure sensation, but he ignored them. He came close, though, and closer still with each sure stroke, making her quiver in anticipation.

She looked down to see her small breasts just filling his hands, his thumbs and fingers bracketing the stiff, aching peaks. Her pent-up breath escaped in a ragged sigh and she moved restlessly, sloshing water out of the tub.

He asked, "Did I hurt you?" A sham question, she knew, calculated to strip away the illusion that she was unaffected, unreachable.

"No," she whispered, meeting his gaze with a frank, if silent, plea. Urging him to call on his own self-control. Lord knew she didn't have the strength to stop him.

He seemed to contemplate her unspoken request, studying her face for long moments, his hands still cupping her. Finally he leaned forward, slowly, so slowly. She felt his heat, drew the intoxicating essence of him deep into her lungs. He smelled of fresh sweat and hard work, a clean, healthy, masculine scent.

His breath teased her before he touched his lips to hers. The first delicate contact electrified her. It was airy. Almost weightless. Yet somehow more intimate than his bold touch. He angled his head, as if testing the shape of her mouth, plucking at it lightly with his mobile lips. She struggled to remain still, chagrined by her weakness, both enthralled and terrified by this power he had over her.

Her agitated breathing made it feel as if he were tugging at her breasts, though his hands remained still. Every little movement sent a jolt of raw sensation through her.

He seemed unconcerned by her lack of response. He continued the dizzying, exploratory kiss, making no move to deepen it. She trembled with the effort to keep from pulling him down and devouring his mouth.

At last, just when she thought she'd reached the limits of her endurance, he sealed his lips over hers, then captured her burning nipples between his fingers. She leaped half out of the tub with a sharp cry, the sound smothered by his mouth. She continued to moan helplessly, clutching at his arms as he pinched and plucked and tormented the sensitized buds.

Finally, when her moans had turned to breathless

pants, he lifted his head and stared into her eyes. *Only I can do this to you,* they seemed to say. *In this way you'll always belong to me.*

He held her gaze as his hand slowly glided down her abdomen and beneath the surface of the water. She lay quiescent and yielding, her body half supported by the warm water, her defenses lulled by a drugging, dreamlike lethargy.

His fingers pushed into the tangle of hair and traced the shape of her feminine mound. Her legs opened for him, an involuntary response she didn't try to fight. His fingertips slid over the swollen cleft and she gasped, her body bowing sharply. It was practically more than she could bear, the sensation so refined, so exquisite, it was close to torture.

He parted her. "You're so wet," he murmured, stroking the slick furrow, his fingers surprisingly cool in contrast to the warm water. Her hips rocked in time to his rhythmic caress. His eyes darkened, the blue of the iris a thin ring around the distended pupil.

She was mesmerized by those eyes, by the smooth, sinewy movement of his shoulder and arm as he touched her. She felt him probe and stretch the opening, and two fingers began to burrow into her. They felt thick and rough and unyielding. With a whimper of pleasure she gripped the sides of the tub and levered herself up to give him better access.

He lifted her near leg over the side of the tub. His fingers twisted, testing the slippery passage. "You're tight," he breathed. "You're so tight, honey."

His eyes searched hers, seeking the answer to an

unspoken question. Finally he asked, "Has the counselor been neglecting you?"

This wasn't the time for lies. "We haven't...we've never..."

She almost laughed at his dumbfounded expression.

"We're...waiting till we're married."

He shook his head, with a little smile of wonder. "You live long enough, you see everything."

She detected a good dose of masculine satisfaction along with the incredulity. She had a stinging comeback all ready, but then he started doing wondrous things with his thumb, while those long, talented fingers advanced and retreated, and she couldn't remember what she'd wanted to say. Within seconds her climax loomed, just out of her grasp.

She panicked. This illicit act was nothing short of betrayal. Infidelity. She was violating one of the cornerstones of her personal value system.

Jack must have sensed her misgivings. He leaned in close and smoothed her wet hair off her face with his free hand. "Don't fight it, Meg. Let it happen."

She whipped her head from side to side, whether from passion or fear, even she couldn't say. Perhaps it was an unholy mixture of both.

He persisted, "I know you. The more you fight it, the more explosive it'll be when it happens." His smile was both amused and salacious. "Which I personally have no problem with, though you might end up screaming the house down." He kissed her open, panting mouth. "Come on, honey. Come for me."

"Don't make me do this. It's wrong...."

She didn't realize she'd said the words aloud until she felt Jack's hand go still, though her body still writhed against it. He just stared at her for a long, charged moment, then withdrew his fingers. He eased her leg back into the tub and stood. His erection strained the fly of his jeans.

Shakily she sat and wrapped her arms around her knees, battling a witch's brew of emotions: shame, self-loathing and remorseless yearning. Her body still hummed and pulsed, though release was no longer in the picture.

She stared straight ahead. In her peripheral vision she saw him yank on his shirt. "We have to stop meeting like this," he muttered, his tone more bitter than droll.

"Did I invite you in here? Either time?"

He didn't answer, but leaned down to drag his fingertips across her chest. "You've got that raggedy flush you get when you're aroused. Better give it a few minutes before you go out and face the guy you're saving it for. Unless you want him to wonder what you've been up to without him."

She hugged herself tighter. "Get out," she snapped, her voice hoarse with unshed tears. She sensed his eyes on her, sensed his hesitation. Her chin trembled. She would not break down in front of him. She'd shown enough weakness for one day.

"Go, Jack. Please."

He sighed. "We'll talk later," he said quietly.

When she didn't respond, he crossed to the door,

opened it a notch to peer into the hallway, and slipped out.

Her eyes squeezed shut and hot tears streaked down her face. "I was over you, dammit," she whispered. "Over you!"

If she said it enough, maybe she'd begin to believe it.

7

"MY *WHAT*?"

"Your saddlebags, darling," Winston said pleasantly. He sat next to Meg on the sofa and gave her jeans-clad thigh a brisk pat. "You've been rather sedentary since our arrival, and I thought you might enjoy a bracing walk in the evening air to work off that turkey sandwich."

"And my saddlebags." Since when did she have fat thighs?

Daisy squirmed on her lap, a Dr. Seuss book clutched in her hands. "Where are your saddlebags, Mommy? I wanna see your saddlebags!"

Jack was leaning against the stone mantel watching Marie and Nora sprawled on the braided rug, playing Scrabble Junior. He glanced at Meg, his expression bland. Too bland. She knew he was eavesdropping.

"My flabby thighs will have to wait," Meg said tightly. "I promised Daisy we'd read her favorite story, *The 500 Hats of Bartholomew Cubbins*."

Daisy bounced on her lap. "I wanna see your saddlebags!"

Winston chucked the little girl under her chin. "You'll have ample opportunity to see them, my dear. They'll get bigger and bigger if Mommy keeps procrastinating this way. We'll just have to remind her again later, won't we?"

What the devil had gotten into him? Meg felt Jack's gaze on her. He quickly returned his attention to the Scrabble game, one hand covering his mouth in a contemplative pose, as if he was fascinated by the tiles Nora was arranging on the playing board. Something about this whole thing didn't scan.

Marie said, "*Stupid* is spelled with a *u*, not two *o*'s, stupid!"

"I'm not stupid!"

Jack said, "Marie, is that the way to help your sister learn how to spell? You promised to be patient when you asked her to play with you."

Nora said, "I don't want to play with stupid Marie!"

Contrition softened Marie's features. "I'm sorry, Nora."

"*Stupid!*"

Jack caught Meg's eye, and they shared a look that made the last two years melt away. Exasperation, amusement and saintlike patience were all rolled into one little lopsided smile. Just like the old days.

Not sparing a glance for Winston, she said, "Mommy's body-sculpting session will have to wait. We have a story to read." She settled Daisy in her arms and opened the book. "'In the beginning, Bartholomew Cubbins didn't have five hundred hats. He had...'" She paused expectantly.

"'Only one hat'!" Daisy chimed in, her chubby finger more or less following the type on the page.

Winston said, "Didn't you read that story to her yesterday?"

Her fingers tightened on the book. "Yes."

"Well, darling, don't you think you should offer the child some variety? As I understand it, the scope of children's literature nowadays is truly remarkable. Certainly you can find something more educational than this fanciful tale written in..." He pried the book from her hands and flipped to the copyright page. "My word—1938! Fourteen years before I was born!"

"No! That ancient?" Meg yanked the book back. "I don't expect you to know this, Winston, but repetition helps to develop a child's reading skills. Children become attached to particular stories and they want to hear them over and over. According to the experts, that should be encouraged."

Winston looked skeptical, but he didn't pursue the issue.

"Where were we, Daisy?" With quick, jerky movements she found their place and continued reading. "'He had only one hat. It was an old one that had belonged to his father...'"

"'And his father's father'!" Daisy continued.

"Meg..."

"*What now?*" She wheeled on Winston.

He waggled a finger at her left hand, which was agitatedly twirling a strand of hair. "I find that mild— I find that annoying, your playing with your hair like that. Of course, I know it can be difficult to relinquish habits of long standing."

"So you've decided to help me."

"Well, yes."

"Well, don't."

For some reason, he glanced at Jack, who just then seemed to find the Scrabble board of immense interest. Winston arched an eyebrow at Meg, his tone stern. "If you persist in this slovenly habit, I certainly will remind you, make no mistake."

Slovenly?

That did it. Meg didn't know why her fiancé had suddenly become her own personal self-improvement gestapo, and at the moment she didn't want to know. She stood and deposited Daisy in his lap. "Mr. Kent wants you to read your favorite book to him, sweetheart. Mommy's going for a walk to burn off those huge, blubbery saddlebags. *Alone.*"

She stalked to the pegs near the front door, grabbed her white anorak and jammed her arms into the sleeves on her way out.

When the door slammed behind her, Winston glanced helplessly at Jack. The poor guy looked shellshocked.

Jack knew he should take pity and let him in on the joke. It was the only decent thing to do. Instead he mouthed, *It's an act—she loves it!* and offered an encouraging thumbs-up.

What was it they said about love and war?

Daisy was puffed with pride. "I'm weading to Mr. Kent, Daddy."

"What a treat," Jack said. "Is it a long book?"

"Uh-huh. *Weal* long. Lots of words!"

"Lucky Mr. Kent."

Upstairs, Tanya ambled out of her room, followed by a rumpled-looking Neal. She homed in on Jack instantly, her greedy gaze about as easy to ignore as jock itch. She moved sluggishly down the steps while Neal remained in the hallway, leaning on the railing and perusing the homey scene below. In his hand was the ubiquitous tumbler of bourbon.

Daisy was "reading" *Bartholomew Cubbins* with great zeal, running her finger along the words and recognizing enough of them to prod her memory. Winston held her gingerly, throwing occasional glances at the door through which Meg had disappeared.

Daisy said, "Look, Mr. Kent." She shoved an illustration in his face. "More hats and more hats. The king is angwy! Look. *Look!*"

"Yes. Quite a rascal, that Bartholomew." He discreetly thumbed ahead to check the length of the book, and sighed.

Tanya sidled up to Jack. "You've been avoiding me."

"Damn right." He was past the point of trying to spare this woman's feelings—if she had any. Tanya Stanton gave new meaning to the term shameless hussy.

She inched closer, backing him against the stone fireplace. Her heavy, spicy perfume had all the subtlety of a pesticide bomb. "We need to talk. In private," she added, with a significant look.

"Nonsense. I wouldn't dream of intruding on your grief." He glanced up to the hallway, where Neal was sipping his bourbon and studying them with flat, sullen eyes. "I'll let those of you who were closest to the dearly departed console each other."

Her smirk told him she recognized sarcasm when she heard it. "If it bothers you to see me with him, then do something about it," she challenged.

He steered her away from the girls. Their aunt Tanya might not care what they heard, but he sure as hell did.

She continued, "You're a man of action, after all. I said it last night, and you proved it, didn't you?"

Marie looked up from her game. "Daddy, is *sol* a word? *S-o-l?*"

"It means your spirit," Nora said gravely. "Like Uncle Pete's soul is in heaven."

Jack said, "That's *s-o-u-l*, sweetheart, but *s-o-l* is a word, too, so you can use it. It's a kind of musical tone." For Tanya's ears only, he ordered, "Keep your distance."

She sighed. "Maybe that is best, for now. I guess we have to be discreet. I just wanted you to know I've taken steps. Things are going to work out." She left him with a sly smile. He reviewed her cryptic words and wondered what nasty surprises were in store for him.

Winston and Daisy had their heads together in the book. Jack quietly walked across the room and lifted his denim jacket off a peg. As he slipped out the door he heard Winston remark, "My word! The king can't mean to have that young fellow beheaded, simply for failing to remove his hat. Why, that's barbaric!"

Sounds to me like the kid needs a good lawyer, Counselor.

Jack buttoned his jacket over his sweater and shoved his hands in his pockets. The cold, sea-scented breeze whipped his hair and went right through his clothes. He crossed the shadowy lawn, grateful for the nearly full moon.

He reached the top of the log steps and scanned the dark beach. The bay was calm tonight. Gentle waves slapped the sand in a rhythm as ancient as the earth. Moonlight puddled on the inky surface of the water, shimmying fingers of quicksilver drawing his eye to the horizon and the unseen north fork of Long Island a mile or so away. Reminding him there was a world beyond this little pimple of land and its troubled inhabitants.

He'd always found the sights and smells and sounds of the shore soothing, as had Meg. He wondered if Winston knew that about her.

The gleam of her windblown hair and white jacket gave her away. She stood on the far end of the rock jetty that jutted into the bay, her back to him. She looked like a shimmering angel, hovering over the water.

Jack made his way down the rustic staircase and across the sand. On the jetty, he stepped carefully from one slick rock to the next, until he was about twenty feet from her. Then he stopped, suddenly loath to intrude on her solitary peace. He was no longer her life partner, after all, but a burden to be borne. The *ex-husband*. A mistake she'd be just as happy to forget if it weren't for the children.

He'd started to retreat when the sound of his name

brought his head up. She half turned; her pale profile seemed to absorb the cool moonlight.

"Don't go," she said.

How had she known he was there? She couldn't have heard him approach, over the wind and waves. Perhaps she'd simply sensed him, as attuned to his presence as he was to hers. His smile was grim as he negotiated the remaining distance to her. *You're projecting again, Wolf. Pathetic.*

They stood side by side on the tip of the jetty, without touching. Waves spanked the rocks at their feet, erupting in a fine mist. The stiff breeze buffeted them, snapping their jackets, tugging their hair.

They didn't speak for a long while. Standing there next to the only woman he'd ever loved, feeling the pull of the fat moon and the lull of nature's primal rhythms, Jack could almost believe his life was happy and complete.

Finally Meg said, "I'm glad you came out here. I was hoping you would."

"Are you sure about that? You know what happens when I get you around water."

A little smile curved her mouth, then faded as she said, "Do you think the phone will come back on before Sunday?"

"Who can say? As far as I know, the phone line doesn't piggyback on the electrical cable—it's separate. There's no telling how long it'll take to restore service."

She stared out over the bay. "I hate to think of Uncle

Pete in that boathouse. I just want this whole thing to be over."

"It will be, soon."

She grimaced. "Another day and a half, if the phones stay out. That charter boat is scheduled to return around noon Sunday."

They lapsed into silence. After a minute Jack felt Meg's eyes on him, felt the disquiet lurking behind them. He said, "Let's have it."

"What?"

"Whatever it is that's eating you. What've I done now?"

She took a deep breath. "I want you to tell me if you've been up in the attic."

His heart did a painful little flip. "Why? Something up there I should see?"

"Can you just answer my question?"

Had he ever directly lied to Meg before? He didn't think so. He would remember feeling this wretched. He made himself look her in the eye. "I've never gone up there. There's never been a reason. The closest I've come is halfway up the stairs when we moved Pete. Why?"

Her expression was solemn, perhaps sad, as she studied him in the moonlight. She slumped a little and turned away, as if she saw through the lie.

That was impossible. How could she know?

She said, "Well, I did go up there. After Pete...after you guys moved him. I found a baseball bat."

After a moment he said, "I see."

"There's..." She shrugged. "There's nothing suspicious about it, per se. It's just an old wooden bat."

"Under the circumstances, I'd say that's suspicious enough. What made you think I might've been up there?"

She shrugged again, not looking at him.

He reached for her shoulder and made her face him. "Say what's on your mind, Meg." His voice was harsher than he'd intended.

She tried to twist away, and he seized both her shoulders.

"You think it was me," he said, gripping her harder. "You think I killed him." She closed her eyes. He shook her. "Say it! It's what you're thinking. Say it!"

The pain stunned him, rolling through him in a scalding wave. She believed this about him. That he was capable of murder. His Meg.

He released her roughly, and caught her arm when her sneaker skidded on the slippery rock.

His voice was flat. "It's because I served time. Hell, I'm an ex-con. I'm capable of anything, right?"

"No. I don't believe that." Her chin trembled.

He faced her squarely, his chest working like a bellows. "Are you afraid of me, Meg?"

"No! No, Jack, of course not!" Her eyes were brimming. "How could I be afraid of you, after all we've been to each other? You're...you're the father of my children."

"I threatened him. You heard me. Everyone did."

She shook her head. "I don't care. You could never

do something like that. It's just not in you. It's not in the man I—'' She stopped abruptly.

He practically reeled from the dizzying rush of relief. He lifted her delicate hands. They were cold as ice. He chafed them between his palms. "I won't deny I hated him, Meg. The man took so much from me. At the moment I made that threat, *I* believed myself capable of it."

She said, "But you aren't. You could never have followed through."

He smiled sadly. "It seems you have more faith in me than I have in myself." He kissed her knuckles and released her hands.

She jammed them in her jacket pockets and stared at the moon-flecked bay. "I'm ready to hear about it."

"About what?"

"You know."

Now that she was willing to listen, he didn't know where to start. He scrubbed at his jaw. "I was fifteen. Mitch was twenty-one. I've told you about Mitch."

"The only thing I know about your brother is he's been in and out of jail his whole adult life."

"Mostly in. And unless the parole boards get a lot more lenient, he's not coming out anytime soon. I always looked up to him when I was growing up. Revered him, really. You know my dad abandoned the family before I was born. As far as male role models went, Mitch was it."

"You were impressionable."

"I was impressionable, but I wasn't stupid. The trouble I got into was my own damn fault. I knew what I was doing. Even when I helped hot-wire that Chevy station wagon and kept the motor running while Mitch went into the liquor store with his nine-millimeter. Haywood Discount Liquors, a neighborhood place. Owned by this skinny, frail old guy—about a hundred and three—who looked like he'd keel over in a strong wind. Everyone called him Grandpa."

Meg listened patiently, her expression revealing nothing.

"I was out in the car, watching through the big display window, my palms sweating on the steering wheel..." he grimaced "...my guts turning to jelly. It hit me then, as I watched Mitch in that stupid ski mask, waving that gun in the old man's face. I thought, What am I doing here? It was like I saw my brother clearly for the first time. A small-time punk. A loser."

"Did he...did he shoot the store owner?"

Jack shook his head. "Grandpa reached under the counter and came out with this huge old revolver. An antique. Probably used it fighting the kaiser. Mitch, he just stands there like an idiot, staring down the barrel of this cannon."

"He didn't expect it."

"My brother isn't what you'd call a criminal mastermind. Doesn't deal well with unanticipated glitches."

"Grandpa shot him?"

"Square in the butt, when he was halfway out the door. I jumped out of the car and hauled him into it by his collar. He was howling and swearing and bleeding all over the place. Grandpa was standing in the doorway with that big gun, aiming the thing right at me."

Meg's hand flew to her mouth.

"Then I saw his face change. He recognized me."

"You weren't wearing a mask?"

"No. Meg, I'd known that old man my whole life, from the neighborhood. I'll never forget the way he looked at me when he lowered that gun."

"What happened then?"

"I just drove. Weaving through traffic, crying, screaming at Mitch. He wouldn't let me take him to a hospital. When the cops caught up with us after a whole five minutes or so, I was grateful."

"But you were only fifteen. How could they put you in jail so young?"

"The DA could've opted for family court in my case, but he was trying to cultivate a tough image, wanted to set an example. He prosecuted me in criminal court. I got fifteen to forty-five months. I served the minimum sentence and was on parole for another fifteen months. Fortunately for me, I got youthful-offender treatment."

"What does that mean?"

"My conviction was wiped out. There's no record of it. If I'd spent even one more month behind bars, I wouldn't have been eligible."

"That's why Pete needed a PI to uncover this."

Jack nodded. "He probably hired a detective and sent him sniffing after whatever dirt he could dig up about me. Must've figured he hit the mother lode with this one."

"Just to keep us apart."

"It was his own personal crusade."

After a moment she said, "Have...have you ever done anything else? Since then?"

"Anything illegal, you mean?"

She nodded.

"No. If it wasn't for Mitch, I wouldn't have done what I did back then. That's not an excuse," he added quickly. "I don't have any of those. I just wanted you to understand how it all came about."

"I think I do, now. Thanks for telling me about it."

"Thanks for letting me."

"I should've listened to you yesterday. I was just...in shock."

"I know."

"I've been thinking about it, Jack. I understand why you kept this from me. I mean, it was wrong of you, but I—I do understand."

He knew he shouldn't ask, but he did anyway. "Would it have made a difference? If I'd told you about this when we met?"

"I've asked myself that. I wish I knew the answer. I'd like to say no, it wouldn't have mattered, that I'd have been able to see past it to your positive qualities, but the truth is, I just don't know."

Did she realize what her words implied? That to her, his "positive qualities" eclipsed even the dreadful truth he'd concealed from her? She wasn't as indifferent to him as she wanted to believe.

"Fair enough," he said. "I guess it really doesn't matter anymore."

She started to say something and stopped. After an awkward few moments he broke the silence. "So this baseball bat."

"Yeah?"

"Any idea who might've hit one out of the park last night? Or down the steps, rather."

"I've had a few thoughts on the matter. And you?"

"Oh, I get to go first, is that it?" He found putting his suspicions into words surprisingly unpalatable. This was Meg's family he was maligning, after all.

He said, "Do you remember Thanksgiving day here five years ago? The tussle Neal and his old man got into?"

"How could I forget? Pete had just left Caroline for Tanya. Neal was outraged over his father's treatment of his mother. He was seventeen then. I didn't expect him to take a swing at Pete, though, did you?"

"Yeah, I did, actually. That kid was in a state." Though hampered by age and flab, Pete had had the advantage of a mind unclouded by fury. He'd dodged the blow and decked his son, bloodying the kid's nose in the process.

Meg said, "Neal's calmed down some since then, but I don't think his feelings for his father have improved much."

"He's just gotten more cautious about showing them. He's been doing your basic slow burn for five years. Biding his time, perhaps."

"So that's who you'd put your money on?" Meg asked. "Neal?"

He shrugged. "He's in the catbird seat. Whether or

not Daddy left him anything in his will, he's got a good thing going with Tanya, who we can now assume is a very wealthy woman. Either way, Neal's fiscal future looks promising."

Her expression hardened. "Neal seems to think that catbird seat is getting a little crowded."

"Let him think what he wants. And the same goes for you. If you can really imagine me with that woman, then you don't know me at all, Meg."

"I know what my eyes and ears tell me."

"So to hell with what *I* tell you, right? Tanya Stanton! Like that could happen. The day I get that desperate is the day I become a monk."

He was glad to see doubt replace some of the anger on her lovely face. "Then what was that 'insatiable' business when you thought I was her?" she asked.

"She'd jumped me earlier in the night, trying to play Find the Knockwurst. Only the knockwurst in question had no desire to be found. So there I am, manfully defending my virtue, when who comes sniffing around but our resident angry young man."

"Uh-oh. What did Neal do?"

"He rescued his woman from the vile seducer—that would be me—and hustled her off."

"So when I woke you up, you naturally assumed I was Tanya back for another try," Meg said.

"After servicing her stepson for an hour or two. You see where I'm going with this."

"Insatiable."

"I rest my case."

"You know, she's just as viable a suspect as Neal.

How long do you think it would've taken before Pete figured out what she was up to?"

"I have to believe he suspected. No one can be that dense."

Meg said, "But why would she take his ring? She's going to get everything anyway—minus whatever he might've left to Neal."

"I don't know about her, but I could see Neal taking it, after doing in the old man. Sort of like adding insult to injury. Or maybe it was simple greed. Fast cash. That diamond must be worth a bundle."

"Could be they're both guilty," Meg said. "Maybe they joined forces to murder him. Did you think of that?"

"I don't know, I can't picture it. When it comes to criminal genius, those two would make my brother look like Lex Luthor."

"I didn't say they'd be *good* at it, just that I wouldn't put it past them to cook up a murderous scheme. She could've lured him up to the attic, and he could've hit him over the head with the bat."

"Why?"

"Why what?"

"Why would they choose the attic?"

"To make it look like an accident when he goes down the stairs."

"And why the middle of the night?"

"Potential witnesses are all sound asleep. Although..." She shivered.

"What?"

"I think I heard something. About the time it happened. I think I heard him falling down the stairs."

Jack swore softly.

"Only I thought it was part of my dream," she added.

"What was happening in your dream?"

Her gaze slid away. "I don't remember."

"What time was that, do you know?"

She squinched her face, thinking. "About one?"

"Not long after my run-in with Tanya and Neal."

"Maybe they didn't start messing around when they left you. Maybe they decided it was time to finish off Uncle Pete."

"They headed for the den. But then, they could've snuck upstairs a minute later. I fell into a dead sleep right away. I'd been awake about thirty-six hours— drove all night to make the boat yesterday morning."

"Which explains why you didn't hear anything when Pete fell down the stairs."

He nodded. "I was *out*. I don't get this 'luring' part of your scenario. How could Tanya possibly entice Pete to go up to the attic in the middle of the night?"

"Something kinky?"

He let his dubious expression say it all.

Meg pushed her wind-whipped hair out of her face. "Okay, then. Maybe she tells him she hears suspicious noises up there. She wants him to go check it out."

"And attentive, devoted husband that he is, he hops right out of bed to do her bidding."

She conceded the point with a wry smile. "Okay. You have any other ideas?"

"Yeah. It was an accident—maybe a heart attack. He fell down the stairs, banged his head. No malice aforethought. No Louisville Slugger."

"What was he doing up there?"

"Maybe he keeps his mean pills in the safe. He was getting his daily dose."

"How'd you know there's a safe up there?"

Damn!

"You did say you've never been in the attic?" she persisted.

"Someone mentioned the safe once. Maybe you."

"No," she said flatly. "I didn't. I know you were up there, Jack. I found one of your sunflower seeds."

He shrugged, thinking fast. "Someone probably tracked it up to the attic on the bottom of their shoe." Time to change the subject. "So tell me. What made you and the counselor decide to wait for the wedding night? Please don't tell me the guy's a forty-five-year-old virgin."

She chuckled. "Quite the opposite, actually. Winston has had a very active sex life."

"Winston?"

"Is that so hard to believe?"

He thought about it. "Yes. I can't picture that fop as a swordsman. No offense."

She grinned wickedly. "I guess Mother never told him not to. He's been going at it since he was fifteen."

Thirty years to perfect his technique. Meg was going to marry a man who'd been seducing women when her first husband was in diapers. Suddenly Jack didn't feel quite so smug about the counselor's advanced years.

She said, "Anyway, he's been careful, of course, but in today's health climate...well, you can't be too careful. He offered to get a blood test, which came back negative, but it can take a long time for the antibodies to show up. He's going to get another test in six months—right before the wedding."

"And meanwhile he takes a lot of cold showers."

"He's been celibate since we started seeing each other."

"Hey, I waited for you, too, remember? *Eight* months." This was a woman any man would wait for. The breeze lifted her hair. He caught the strands and tucked them behind her ear, adding softly, "You have a way of narrowing a guy's focus."

She looked up at him, her expression heartbreakingly candid, almost shy. She was gauging his sincerity, he knew. And he let her see it, that and so much more—all the love and longing he'd tried so hard to disown. She dropped her eyes, but not before he saw her self-doubt, her confusion.

Good. He wanted her confused. He wanted her to question every move she made, every step that took her further from him.

So quietly he had to lean close to hear her over the wind, she said, "You're the only man I've slept with."

He wanted to kiss her then, her face was right there, her lips, that beautiful mouth. He wanted to drag her into his arms and claim her, possess her, stamp her as his. Take her right there on the slick rocks under the fat, swaggering moon and howl his triumph across the bay.

She was still his, in this elemental way. He was still the only man she'd ever given herself to, the only man who'd touched her and cherished her and filled her, body and soul.

She whispered, "I wanted you to know that."

He swallowed a knot of emotion. "I'm glad."

She looked away. "I don't expect it's the same for you. I mean, it's been two years. I know there must've been...women."

In that instant he wished there hadn't been. Just to erase that haunted look from her eyes. But he wouldn't lie. "A few," he said quietly. "No one you know."

She nodded stiffly, still not looking at him. She tried to smile, but it was a dismal effort. "I had no right to ask."

He reached for her arm, and dropped his hand without touching her. He wanted to make her smile for real. "Did I tell you I'm buying a house?"

It took a moment for her mind to switch gears. Then her eyebrows shot up. "A *house*? How can you—" She clamped her mouth shut.

"How can I afford it? You mean, living hand-to-mouth the way I do?"

She started to twist a strand of hair, but the wind frustrated her. "I just meant..."

"I know what you meant. Meg honey, I wasn't kidding when I told you the pub's doing well. It's *the* hip spot in town. You should see it on the weekends—

wall-to-wall customers. People waiting an hour for a table."

"You and Kevin are actually making money?"

"Serious money. We're plowing a lot of it back into the business, of course. We're even scouting around for a second location—Wolf Mann Brew Pub Two. And in the meantime, my savings account's getting fat and I was able to put a hefty down payment on the house."

"That's great, but..."

"But what?"

"Well, it's so...precarious, a pub. Dependent on the whims of a fickle public. A competing business could open up around the corner tomorrow. It could all fall apart like that, everything you've worked so hard for."

"You make it sound like one of Ralph Kramden's wacky schemes. We're well capitalized. We've planned for contingencies. We keep on top of the trends." He couldn't keep the hurt out of his voice. "If you'd ever shown an interest in the business, you'd know that.

"Look," he continued, "I've never denied there's an element of risk. But that risk decreases every month we stay in the black. I'm building a cushion, Meg. I'm building a future." *I wish to God you were still part of it.*

"It's still not as secure as a regular paycheck." It was her old refrain, but something told him her heart was no longer in it.

"Meg, think about it. Look what's happening to all those people we know who work for big corporations.

They're getting laid off. Or, excuse me, 'downsized.' Every week another buddy of mine is out of work. There are no guarantees. Whether you work for yourself or someone else."

She hugged herself. "It's all I ever wanted," she said, her voice so small he had to strain to hear her. "Stability. You don't know what it was like, growing up the way I did."

He stepped closer and pushed her hair off her cold face. He brushed his hand down her cheek and lifted her chin. With a gentle smile he said, "Do you remember that house on the corner of Arlington and Fox? That big old yellow Victorian we used to park in front of and stare at and fantasize about?"

"Yeah..."

"I bought it."

Her jaw dropped. "You didn't! How could you—"

He laughed. "If you ask me one more time how I can afford it, I'll feed you to the sharks. I can. Trust me." He added quietly, "Just trust me, Meg. It's all I ever asked."

Her eyes filled as she stared at him. "I know," she whispered.

He caressed her jaw and pushed his fingers into the hair at her nape. It felt like silk, like silver gossamer floating on the breeze. "I always promised I'd never let you down. I never said it would be easy. But I promised to take care of you and the kids, and I always did."

"Yes," she admitted, "you always did." Her expression pleaded for understanding. "I was so scared, Jack."

"I know you were, honey. I guess I didn't know just how scared, though. I mean, it was so clear to me that we were going to be okay, I figured how could she not see it? But..." He sighed. "I knew how rough you had it as a kid. Maybe I should've done more to make you feel secure."

"I don't know if anything could've made me feel secure." She leaned into him, and he wrapped his arms around her, resting his cheek on her cool, fragrant hair. "I was so terrified of ending up like my mother, it was like I had blinders on. I couldn't see what was so obvious to you."

"The light at the end of the tunnel."

"All I could see was the tunnel."

This was as close as she'd ever come to admitting she'd made the wrong choice. Jack tightened his arms around her and tried not to read too much into her words. Hope, he'd already discovered, was a treacherous emotion.

8

"MOMMY AND MR. KENT are yelling."

"I can hear that, sweetheart." Jack slid Marie's breakfast onto her plate—her custom-ordered Daddy's Special Pancake, shaped to her specifications. When he'd constructed his first pancake bunny years ago, thus instituting a family tradition, he couldn't have guessed that one day he'd find himself trying to fashion a unicorn out of Aunt Jemima batter.

"What's that?" she asked, pointing.

"That's its horn." He studied the misshapen lump of batter extending from the horse's head. "It's having a bad-horn day. What'll it be, Nora?"

Daisy already had her turtle. Turtles he had down. They took all of about ten seconds. Big blob, foot, foot, foot, foot, head, little pointy tail.

"I want an angel," Nora said. "Like Uncle Pete. He's an angel now."

Jack ruffled her hair tenderly, thinking that if he was going to craft Uncle Pete in pancake batter, he'd better practice those horns. And forked tails, while he was at it. "An angel it is."

An especially vociferous screech from the living room brought everyone's head up. It was just as well they couldn't make out Meg's exact words—although a few snippets did rocket through the door. *Pompous! Overbearing! Nitpicky!* Plus a smattering of those choice terms sure to curdle Mother Kent's Geritol.

"Daddy, why are you smiling?" Marie asked.

"Oh, I'm just happy to be with my girls." Batter sizzled in the pan as he poured out an angel with less-than-symmetrical wings. Its halo looked more like a sombrero.

After a minute he flipped his creation, one ear cocked to the escalating squabble in the living room. Winston didn't strike him as the type to lose his cool, much less get physical with a woman. Nevertheless, Jack deemed it prudent to pull in the reins. The girls had already gotten an earful; enough was enough. His little practical joke had probably outlived its amusement potential, anyway.

Too bad. It was fun while it lasted.

He quickly deposited Nora's south-of-the-border angel on her plate and pushed through the doorway. The combatants were facing off near the far wall, next to the mantel: Meg flushed with anger, fists planted on her hips; her betrothed in a posture of supreme arrogance, arms crossed over his chest.

She snapped, "Give me some credit, Winston. What are you afraid I'll say when you introduce me to your mother? 'How the hell are you, Mrs. Kent, I'm damn proud to be marrying your son'?"

"When I'm satisfied that you've expunged such slatternly words from your vocabulary, then I'll—"

"*Slatternly?*"

"Then I'll consider introducing you to Mother."

She got right in his face, forcing him to back up to the wall. Jack was gratified to see her venting her temper on someone else, especially this particular someone else. He hung back, knowing they were unaware of his presence.

She poked a finger in Winston's chest. "If *you* stop acting like such a prissy old maid, then *I* might consider going through with this marriage!"

"Such name-calling is unbecoming, Meg." He smiled suggestively. "And so pointless, when you and I both know how *turned on* you are right now."

Jack thought if her jaw dropped any lower, it would dislocate. She struggled to say something, but appeared to be choking on her outrage.

Winston added, "I'll show you just how much of a 'prissy old maid' I am on our wedding night, darling."

He reached for her. She batted his hand away. He balled his fist. In the heartbeat of time it took Jack to spring across the room, Winston had pivoted and smashed his knuckles into the wall.

And recoiled instantly, clutching his hand, his face contorted in a rictus of agony. The wall was unscathed.

Meg wheeled around and collided with Jack, shoved past him, sprinted up the stairs and disappeared into her room. The door slammed.

Meanwhile Winston was doing a little rain dance, stomping around in a circle, hunched over. Finally he ground to a halt, took a long, wheezing breath and swore savagely at the wall.

Jack said, "It's broken."

"Nonsense. There's not a scratch on the damn thing."

"Not the wall. Your hand."

Winston gaped at him, then stared at the appendage, gingerly unclenching his fingers. Jack examined the smashed knuckle at the base of Winston's pinkie, already swelling alarmingly. "This is what they call a boxer's break. And that's a surefire way to get it, trying to put your fist through a solid wall."

"But you—but you...!" Winston gestured at the neat hole Jack had made in the adjacent wall two days before.

So that was it. The poor sap had been at it again, trying to prove to the love of his life that he was every inch the macho man her ex was.

Jack said, "You don't know much about house construction, do you?" Winston's only response was a dark glower. "You see, that wall—" Jack pointed to the newly ventilated one "—is only four years old. It's plasterboard. This living room was a lot bigger before Tanya decided she needed a den. See there? Those two sconces are hung on the studs. I knew if I aimed between them, I'd hit nothing but Sheetrock. Felt damn good, too."

"And I hit a stud," Winston growled.

"Maybe, maybe not. See, you went after an outside wall, original to the house. Back then they used plaster over wooden lath. No matter where you hit it, that wall's gonna win. You really don't know this stuff?"

Winston responded with an expletive Jack knew he hadn't learned from Meg. Perhaps now wasn't the best time to let him in on the joke that had started this whole debacle.

Jack said, "Better ice that sucker. Let's see what we can scare up in the way of a sling."

"FETCH ME THE AFGHAN, would you, darling?" Winston gestured with the bottle of single-malt Scotch he'd been methodically draining for the last three hours. At some point he'd abandoned his glass and started swigging straight from the bottle of very old, very expensive whiskey, which had sat unopened in the liquor cabinet for about thirty years, a gift from some long-ago visitor. Pete hadn't been a Scotch drinker.

Winston lay sprawled on the living room sofa, propped up with pillows. His plaid flannel shirt was half-untucked, his hair disheveled. Tanya's *Cosmopolitan* magazine served as a makeshift splint, cradling his arm, which was further supported in a sling fashioned from one of her silk scarves. A plastic bag of ice lay on the swollen knuckle.

As Meg passed him she bestowed her best imitation of a casual smile. "Let me take that for you. I'll bring you a sandwich." She reached for the whiskey bottle.

He jerked it out of her reach and stared up at her, his eyes glassy and unfocused. "Just the afghan for now. I couldn't eat a bite." He seemed to be overenunciating, obviously compensating for his thick tongue.

Gritting her teeth, she retrieved the afghan from an easy chair. Jack stood in his usual spot leaning against the mantel, munching his ubiquitous sunflower seeds and watching her fetch and carry for her foolish show-off of a fiancé.

She knew perfectly well why Winston had punched the wall. She supposed she should be flattered. However, she couldn't help feeling that for all her fiancé's self-professed maturity and prudence, he could be incredibly insecure at times. This childish stunt was the direct result of that insecurity.

She didn't care for the misgivings creeping into her mind, undermining her well-laid plans. She'd had it all worked out—her whole future, her children's future. She thought of all the pain she'd endured the last few years, the emotional turmoil. The strength of will it had taken for her to leave a man she loved, and start life over.

This was the only life she was going to get. She had one chance to do it right. And so she'd taken steps. She'd undone her one big mistake: marrying Jack Wolf. So why did she feel cheated?

"Do take care, darling. My hand!"

She'd been tucking the afghan around Winston with a bit more fervor than the task required. Sighing, she straightened. "Winston, I really wish you'd give me that bottle."

He glared at her with startling malevolence. "I never realized nagging was one of your myriad shortcomings. Seems I'm learning new things about you every day, darling."

She was stunned by how deeply his words hurt. Humiliation twisted her stomach and burned her eyes. She struggled to keep her expression neutral.

She felt Jack's eyes on her and wanted to crawl under the braided rug. She didn't dare look at him, afraid she'd see the smugness he had every right to feel at that moment. He had to be laughing at her, glorying in Winston's taunting words. After all, wasn't that what she'd done to Jack—nagged him incessantly to abandon his reckless dreams and settle down?

She tried to remind herself that Winston was in pain. That was the only reason he'd resorted to copious quantities of booze, after all, when she'd never before seen him take more than a few sips of wine. She'd almost forgiven him his cruel gibe when his good arm whipped out and slapped her playfully on the butt.

"But I think I'll keep you!" he hollered.

Before he could see the hurt in her eyes, she turned away. In that instant she wanted nothing more than to yank the ostentatious rock off her ring finger and throw it in his face.

Supposedly alcohol broke down a person's inhibitions. Was this petulant, mean-spirited boor the genuine article, then—the real man beneath the veneer of urbane sophistication Winston presented to the world?

Heaven help her.

Jack's gaze drew her in against her will. The mocking smile she'd expected was absent. To Winston his expression must have appeared bland, even bored. But she knew Jack as no other, and what she read beneath the surface made fresh tears spring to her eyes. It was all there, everything he felt for her. Respect. Concern. Love.

She knew it then, as clearly as she'd ever known anything. He loved her. He always had.

Had she given up on the two of them too easily? Had she allowed her irrational fears to rob her of the one great joy in her life?

During the past two years she'd made great strides in her career. She should have been deliriously happy. Wasn't that what she'd always wanted—financial stability? But at the same time, she'd never felt more adrift, more incomplete. Her success meant nothing without Jack to share it with.

Countless times she'd craved his steady presence. She'd longed to see his face break into a proud grin at every little milestone, no matter how trivial. Longed to bask in the comfort of his loving support during the occasional setback.

But she'd given it up. Given *him* up. Her choice. She'd learned long ago that you can't have everything. Sometimes you have to sacrifice something you want for a greater reward.

She had her reward, but somehow it felt more like a consolation prize.

From the den came the sound of three shrill voices squealing in delight. The girls were watching *A Little Princess* on the VCR. The front door opened and Neal sauntered in. For the hundredth time he asked, "Phones still out?"

Meg wished he'd stop asking and just pick up the receiver himself. "Last time I checked."

He swore and tossed his leather jacket toward a coat hook. It slid to the floor and he left it there. Flopping down in his father's favorite easy chair, he asked his second-favorite question. "Where's Tanya?"

I don't know and I don't care, Meg wanted to answer. "I really couldn't say."

The lady of the house chose that moment to appear at the top of the stairs, blowing on her fresh nail polish—vivid tangerine. She descended the steps. "Give it a rest, Neal. You don't have to keep track of me every second of the day, you know."

Neal's eyes flicked to Jack. "I just like to know what you're up to."

"Oh, don't start." She ambled over to Winston and ran her fingers along his arm over the sling. "How's that hand feeling, Winston?"

"Still hurts like the devil, but thank you for asking, Tanya. It's nice to know *someone* cares."

Meg rolled her eyes.

Tanya perched on the edge of the sofa, and Winston scooted over to make room for her. She tapped the multicolored silk scarf. "Is the sling working out okay?"

"Jus' dandy."

"Do you need more ice? Another pillow?"

"I think I'm set for now."

"How's that Scotch holding out?"

He wagged the half-empty bottle.

Her voice oozed admiration. "I don't know how you endure the agony, Winston, with only a little whiskey to take the edge off. It's times like this that really test a man's virility."

He gazed at her with a big, foolish grin, preening

under her insincere flattery. Meg felt embarrassed for him. She wondered who this little display was meant to impress—Jack or Neal. Perhaps both. Tanya wouldn't be happy until she had every male in the place slavering over her.

She patted his good hand. "You just rest. I'll do everything I can to ease your suffering."

He squeezed her hand. "Jus' knowing you're concerned makes it feel better already."

"Taking care of others helps keep my mind off..." Her chin trembled.

"You're going through your own agony now, my dear. And quite bravely, might I add."

"There are just so many...unanswered questions." She sniffed. "I know I won't have any peace until they're resolved."

Intriguing words from the woman Meg considered Suspect Numero Uno.

Winston said, "You mean questions like what was Pete doing in the attic?"

"That's part of it."

"Well...and then there's the matter of his ring, of course. The missing ring."

Tanya perked up. "That's right. The ring. I just can't get it out of my mind."

"Why, there's only one thing to do," he declared. "We mus' find that ring. If it turns up in someone's personal effects, that would certainly shed some light on this nasty business." He squeezed her hand again. "And give you some peace of mind, my dear."

"Well...if you insist."

Neal sat up straighter. "Are you suggesting we search everyone's stuff?"

"It would seem the sensible course," Winston replied.

Meg said, "Don't you think we should leave that sort of thing to the police?"

"Now that we're talking about it, we've gotta follow through, or whoever has it will stash it somewhere it'll never be found," Tanya pointed out. "No, I agree with Winston. We have to look for it now. All of us together. So no one can pull a fast one."

Neal surprised Meg by agreeing. "Damn straight. Let's get started. Meg?"

She shrugged. What harm could it do? "Okay, I guess."

Jack had been silent. Now she looked at him, wordlessly questioning. What she saw in his expression prickled her scalp.

"No one's touching my duffel," he said. His features were rigid. He refused to look at Meg.

Neal made a grunting noise that indicated he wasn't surprised. Tanya appeared genuinely taken aback. "It's okay, Jack," she said. "Everyone's stuff'll be searched, not just yours." Her eyes widened fractionally. Unless Meg was mistaken, she was sending him a message.

"Forget it," he said. "My things are off-limits."

Meg's chest tightened with foreboding. Why would he refuse to go along? He had to know how guilty his lack of cooperation made him appear.

She knew he hadn't killed Pete. That knowledge

was branded on her heart. She'd never believe him capable of such an act. But could he have taken the ring? Last night he'd told her he hadn't done anything illegal since the bungled holdup that had landed him in jail at age fifteen. She'd believed him.

Dammit, she still did. Whoever took Pete's ring had to have done so before she discovered his body. It could have been anyone.

Winston struggled up from his lounging position, carefully supporting his bad arm. Appearing almost sober, he addressed Jack. "I advise you to reconsider, my friend. Your refusal to cooperate casts you in a...less-than-favorable light."

Meg sensed Winston was dismayed by Jack's resistance, as if he, too, believed in his innocence.

"I'm not worried," Jack said. "I have nothing to hide. I just value my privacy, that's all."

Still Jack wouldn't meet Meg's eyes. She knew this wasn't just an issue of privacy for him.

Winston sighed. "Come along, then. We might as well get this over with."

JACK CHOSE TO ACCOMPANY them during the room-by-room search, prompting Neal's snide observation that apparently the only privacy Jack valued was his own.

They started in Neal's and Winston's room. Clothes were shaken out, laundry bags emptied, toiletry kits pawed through. It didn't take long to come up empty.

"You know," Neal said, eyeing Jack, "any one of us could have the thing in a pocket. Or it could be hidden in one of the other rooms of the house. Even the tool-shed or boathouse."

Tanya scowled at him. "At least this is a start."

They searched Tanya's room next. Meg was baffled as to why one woman would bring so many clothes for a four-day trip. The makeup bag was the size of a small suitcase. Tanya invited Winston to examine her drawerful of lingerie. If he were sober, he probably would have insisted Meg do the honors. As it was, he eagerly applied himself to the task, one-handedly groping his hostess's lacy underwear and filmy night-ies.

"Nothing here," Neal announced at last. "Next stop, Meg's room."

She watched as Neal, Tanya and Winston went through her clothes and toiletries. At that moment she regretted having agreed to participate. *This must be why Jack refused*, she thought, hugging herself against the feeling of violation. She was grateful for his solid, watchful presence beside her.

Winston struggled to unzip her small cosmetic bag, battling his handicap and the whiskey sloshing around in his brain. He shook the contents onto the ecru, crocheted bedspread. Out tumbled her mascara, two lipsticks, powder, blusher and Uncle Pete's ring.

9

MEG'S GASP FROZE the action in a bizarre *tableau vivant.* Winston was a statue, still holding the cosmetic bag over the bed, staring slack jawed at the glittering bauble. As was everyone else.

"My word!"

Meg stood stiff and numb, her arms still wrapped around her middle. Sick dread swamped her and she couldn't form a coherent thought—until she felt Jack's warm palm on her back.

He snarled a promise, meeting everyone's eyes in turn. "I will find out who's responsible for this."

The truth struck her like a punch to the gut. She'd been set up. Framed.

Her mind raced. Who had suggested this search in the first place? Winston. But only for the "grieving" widow's peace of mind. Both Tanya and Neal had been gung ho about the idea.

Jack's arm slid around Meg's shoulders and she realized she was trembling.

Tanya was the picture of stunned betrayal. "Meg...?"

"This is ridiculous," Meg said, but her voice emerged as a quavering whisper. "You know I would never..."

Neal picked up the ring and clenched it in his fist. He shook his head slowly, staring at Meg with dawning awareness. "You found Dad. You were the one who found his body."

Winston asked Neal, "What's that you have there?"

Neal looked down at the sheaf of legal-size papers in his other hand, as if he'd forgotten about them. He nodded at Meg's open suitcase. "I found this in there. It's..." He peered at the first page. "It's Dad's will!"

Meg shot Jack a startled glance. "I've never even seen his will!"

He pulled her against his side. One look at his eyes told her she didn't have to convince him.

Winston took the document from Neal and flipped to the last page. "It's dated November thirteenth—exactly two weeks ago."

Tanya's eyes widened. "He changed his will?"

Neal looked grim. "He never said anything to me."

Scanning the document, struggling to focus, Winston suddenly looked up. Directly at Meg. What she saw in his eyes made her tremble harder. He could have been looking at a stranger. "Pete left everything to Meg," he said.

Tanya cried out and clapped a hand over her mouth. Neal cursed loudly.

Meg said, "I don't believe it."

But she did. Wasn't this exactly the kind of gesture irascible Pete Stanton would have made when confronted with his wife's blatant infidelity and his own son's betrayal? This bequest had nothing to do with how much he loved Meg, and everything to do with how much he hated Tanya and Neal. He wouldn't have hesitated to turn his last will and testament into a tool of retribution against those who'd wronged him.

Poring over the papers, Winston continued, "Meg inherits the homes, the business and all investments. Tanya and Neal are mentioned briefly. Only the diamond ring goes to them, as a joint bequest. Which must explain why Meg—" He halted abruptly.

Her blood pressure soared. "Why I what? Go on, tell me! *Why I took the ring?*"

He didn't answer.

She shook off Jack's arm and took a shaky step toward her fiancé. "Winston? Answer me. Is that what you believe? That I stole Pete's ring?" He met her eyes but said nothing. She felt a painful pressure in her chest.

Neal said, "We're talking about a whole lot more than just a ring here." He snatched the papers from Winston and shook them at her. His nostrils flared and hot color washed his face. "My father's dead, and what convenient timing. You inherit everything, Meg. What rightfully belongs to me and Tanya." He tossed the will on the bed.

Meg said, "You can't believe that I...Neal, for pity's sake. Listen to yourself! I told you, I never saw this will. I had no idea I was even mentioned in it."

"Meg," Jack said. "Don't waste your breath defending yourself. Whoever planted this stuff in your luggage is right here in this room. We'll get to the bottom of it."

Neal sneered, "Good move, Wolf. I'd be sucking up to her now, too, if I were you. Your ex is a millionaire. Better talk your way into her pants again if you haven't alread—"

Neal shrank back a little as Jack advanced on him, and flinched when he laid a big hand on his shoulder.

"You're talking about a lady," Jack said quietly. "Now, I know you don't have much experience with those, so I'm gonna cut you some slack. This time. If you promise to control that nasty mouth of yours."

Neal only glared at him venomously. Jack squeezed his shoulder. The gesture looked downright avuncular, but Neal's wince told Meg it was more along the lines of the Vulcan nerve pinch. "How about it, Neal? You ready to show the lady a little respect?"

"Yeah," he grunted.

Jack patted his shoulder. "You'll learn some manners yet."

Rubbing his shoulder, Neal muttered, "I don't think it was her that killed him, anyway."

"Could've fooled me," Jack said. "Who, then?"

"That one." He nodded toward Winston, who gawked at him, apparently struck speechless.

Neal gestured toward the papers on the bed. "Dad gives Meg a copy of his new will, but it's like their little secret, you know? He doesn't tell me or Tanya. Meg shares the good news with her fiancé here, who starts thinking the hell with that, I'm not waiting around till the old guy decides to croak. Right, Winston?"

"Certainly not!" he sputtered. "She never even told me about the new will!"

"Winston!" Meg cried. "For heaven's sake, I didn't know about it!"

But she'd already said that. He simply didn't believe her. He thought her capable of stealing the ring and possibly of murdering her uncle for the inheritance, as well. As painful as his lack of faith was, she consoled herself with the fact that at least this side of him had revealed itself *before* the wedding.

And that she'd never slept with the pompous jerk.

Tanya said, "I, for one, refuse to believe Winston's involved in this."

"Tanya!" Winston beamed. "The voice of reason. Thank you!"

"Except as Meg's accomplice," she amended.

He reeled from the sucker punch. "Accomplice!"

"After all," Tanya continued, "it was your law firm that drew up this will."

"Hey, yeah, that's right!" Neal said.

Meg saw Jack's speculative gaze home in on Winston. She could almost hear him mentally shuffling this intriguing tidbit into place amid all the other facts and suppositions.

Tanya said, "Isn't that how you met Meg? Through the firm?"

Winston drew himself up, obviously trying to look imposing. "Watkins, Gilroy and Stone has represented Pete for several years, but I never met him in person until Thursday. It's a very large firm and I'm in the real estate area, not estates and taxes. I met Meg at a reception which several of the firm's corporate clients attended."

By his beleaguered expression, she guessed he wished he'd skipped the reception. If so, the feeling was mutual.

Neal persisted, "But you had access to his will. It would've been nothing to snoop around, make a copy of it—"

"But I didn't! Meg, tell them I'm not your accomplice!"

"I don't know," she said, "you look guilty as hell from where I'm standing."

"*Meg!*"

She slipped his engagement ring off her finger and tucked it into his shirt pocket. "Save it for someone less slatternly." She spun on her heel and marched through the doorway.

LEANING ON AN ELBOW, Meg stared through the gloom at the living room hearth. All that remained of the fire that had blazed there earlier in the evening was glowing coals. The faint scent of wood smoke hung in the air. It was well past midnight.

Jack, where are you?

She flopped back onto the sofa and squirmed, trying to straighten the wool blanket and her flannel nightgown, which clung together tenaciously.

She'd lain in her bed upstairs for two hours, her mind and body too restless for sleep. Her heart raced when she thought of Uncle Pete's will.

He'd left her his fortune. It still hadn't sunk in. They

may as well have told her she'd won the lottery. All her money problems, those desperate, long-held fears that had composed such a huge segment of her psyche, were gone in the blink of an eye.

Her heart also raced when she thought of what she'd done.

She'd given Winston back his ring. They were no longer engaged, a circumstance that left her both terrified and immensely relieved. Terrified because she'd pinned so much hope on their upcoming marriage, what was to have been the cornerstone of her new life, the life she'd always wanted—the life she needed, even if financial stability was no longer an issue. Relieved because if she was being honest with herself, she couldn't envision spending the rest of her life living with Winston Kent III, making love with him, raising children with him.

Her thoughts had naturally strayed to Jack then. He was her past. Was he her future, too? Was she destined—doomed—to repeat a destructive pattern? A pattern she'd learned at her mother's knee: unquestioning devotion to a man who could only bring heartache.

She mentally shook herself. No. She could no longer view the situation in those simplistic terms, and it had nothing to do with her sudden inheritance. Jack, with patience and love, had helped her see how she'd allowed baseless fears to cripple her perspective.

Still, she couldn't ignore her instincts, the self-protective impulses that had made her leave him in the first place.

Two years ago her course of action had seemed so clear-cut. Now she struggled for the right answers. But along with confusion came hope, something that had been glaringly absent in her life.

And hope felt good. Scary, but good.

As she thought of Jack, her restlessness took on a new dimension, one she'd become all too familiar with during the past two years. Her physical need for him was so profound, so fundamental, she felt as if a part of herself were missing.

Tomorrow the charter boat would arrive and they'd go their separate ways: she and the girls to their house on Long Island; Jack to Ithaca and the lovely old yellow Victorian that had once fueled their forever-after daydreams.

But for now, they were still here, together, on this island in the middle of the bay. For once, she'd surrendered to impulse. She'd crept downstairs twenty minutes ago, only to find the sofa vacant. She'd settled down to wait for him, a not-quite-virgin sacrifice in a full-length flannel nightgown.

A hysterical giggle erupted from her, the sound unnaturally loud in the still, dark room. She lay motionless, hyperaware of her body, the hectic ticking of her pulse, the rapid rise and fall of her breasts, their hard tips brushing against the thick flannel.

Every inch of her skin was sensitized; she felt every wrinkle in the soft cloth, every fold. The pressure of the blanket, the weight of it, was maddening, settling heavily between her legs and across her chest as if pressed there by an unseen hand.

She jerked as the front door creaked open, admitting a cold, sea-scented breeze. Moonlight outlined Jack's form for scant seconds before the door closed and inky darkness enveloped her once more. His footsteps slowed as he approached the sofa. He sensed her presence, she knew, though the deep shadows concealed her.

She felt his heat close by, strained her eyes in vain. She saw only a vague shape looming over her, felt his warm breath as he bent lower. Cold fingers touched her face, delicately tracing her eyebrows, her nose and jaw. Her lips parted and his fingertips were there, a whispery caress that filled her with the scent of him, the taste of him.

"Jack..." she whispered on a ragged breath. One finger touched her lips admonishingly. He was right. Words had always gotten them into trouble. This wasn't the time for words.

He flung the blanket off her. A sharp pang of desire struck deep and low. It all happened so fast then. And the voice in her head chanted, *Yes yes yes yes—*

His breath fanned her in rapid bursts as he mounted her, pushing her gown to her waist and roughly shoving her legs wide with cold, jeans-clad knees. His open denim jacket tented her body, concentrating his essence, his heat. Belt leather snapped like a whip, the brass buckle startlingly cold where it dragged across her belly. Coarse knuckles brushed her sex as he freed himself. She moaned, straining toward him, clawing his hard waist, all slick, thumping hunger.

His long fingers gripped her buttocks as he drove

into her deep and fast, muffling her cry with his mouth, just like the first time.

And just like the first time, he was thicker, harder, more blatantly virile than she could have imagined. He didn't pause, but gripped her tighter, tilting her hips for his hammering thrusts.

His possession of her mouth mirrored that of her body, his relentless, penetrating kiss forcing her to open to him, to yield to him in every way. She sensed her conscious will softening even as the physical tension within her rose to a crescendo. He relinquished her mouth to whisper a harsh command in her ear.

"Come!"

Her shrill, panting breaths echoed the cadence of his jackhammer thrusts. They were like two halves of a well-oiled machine, moving with precision. His jacket had become a steam tent; his curly hair was damp where it brushed her face. Her knee slammed the back of the sofa repeatedly, but she couldn't care.

"Come, Meg. Now!"

Her mouth opened on a sharp, stunned gasp and his hand covered it, smothering her hoarse cries as her body convulsed under him, around him. He groaned in response and seemed to swell inside her with every shuddering spasm. He pulled her legs up over his shoulders. His hips pistoned hard and fast, lifting her with each pounding stroke.

He reared over her, frozen for one long heartbeat. A drop of sweat landed on her chin and etched a hot trail downward to puddle in the hollow of her throat. He recoiled and plunged, rocking, quivering, jetting into her in hot, pulsing waves. His strangled groan vibrated through her.

He lowered her legs and sank onto her, his weight a welcome burden. Their bodies remained separated by layers of damp, twisted clothing, except where he still pulsed deep within her. His chest heaved, his breath hot on her cheek. His heart pummeled her right through their clothes. She stroked his hair with trembling fingers.

She would never regret this. To her dying day, no matter what the future held, she'd never regret sharing herself with Jack this night, this way.

He snuggled his face close to hers and sighed heavily in her ear. She smiled and felt his answering grin. His eyelashes tickled her as he blinked.

He mumbled, "How much time do you think it's been since I walked through that door? About a minute?"

A chuckle bubbled up from her. "That long?"

"It's like I was...possessed." He angled up on an elbow. "You okay? I wasn't very gentle."

In answer, she pulled him back down. Held him tightly. Whispered, "I need you, Jack."

He smoothed damp strands of hair off her temple and pressed a soft kiss there. "For how long?"

She knew what he wanted to hear. *For always.* She swallowed the words. How could she promise him anything when she didn't know her own mind, when she was so confused? "I can't think beyond tonight," she whispered.

After a few moments he kissed her on the lips, a

simple, cherishing kiss. He eased off her, and she gasped as he withdrew from her body. He zipped his jeans.

"Come." He took her hand and pulled her off the sofa.

"Where?" But she knew.

He led her unerringly through the dark living room, up the stairs and into her room. He switched on the small bedside lamp, bathing the room in a warm glow. Pinning her with his gaze, he shrugged out of his jacket and pitched it onto a chair, then came to stand before her.

He said, "Have I ever told you how much flannel turns me on?" She couldn't take her eyes off his— crystal blue, crinkled at the corners. The erotic promise she read there shot through her like lightning, melting the very heart of her. "Must be some kind of Pavlovian response."

He gathered the heavy material of her nightgown and drew it up and off her, tossing it onto his jacket. His eyes darkened as he stared at her, standing naked before him. He lifted his hand and skimmed it up her side reverently, from her hip to her breast. He molded her soft flesh with his callused fingers.

A twist of longing darted through her. She hissed in a breath. And smiled. "What you do to me..."

Now she could admit it: Winston left her cold. He was a skillful kisser, no question. His practiced caresses had been pleasant, not unwelcome, but they never turned her on. Whereas Jack...

Jack could inflame her with a look.

She reached out and pulled him closer. His mouth descended on hers as his hand slid down her abdomen, into her damp curls and lower. Her breath snagged and she flinched away from his touch, only then realizing how tender she was.

"I hurt you," he said, frowning.

"I'm just a little sore. It's been a long time."

"I was too rough." He cupped her lightly. "I should've—"

"No. It was perfect. You were perfect." She slipped her hands around his neck and kissed him.

"Lie down," he murmured against her mouth.

She wasn't sure what he had in mind, but she obeyed, letting him settle her on the sheets of her rumpled bed.

He said, "Wait here," and left the room. He returned seconds later with a wet washcloth and a towel.

Meg's pulse accelerated as he sat next to her and gently parted her thighs. Carefully, so carefully, he pressed the warm, moist cloth between her legs. Again she was reminded of the first time they'd made love. There'd been a little blood then, and he'd lovingly cleansed her, pampered her, just as he was doing now.

He shifted the compress slightly, applied a little more pressure. "How's that?" he asked.

"Better," she breathed, trying not to squirm under his hand. The warm cloth did ease the burning soreness, but the overall effect was less than calming. His hand looked dark against the white cloth and her pale thighs. All sensation was focused on the subtle movements of his long fingers.

He smiled apologetically. "I'm an animal."

She grinned. "Completely uncivilized."

"When I came in the house and found you there, waiting for me, I think I went a little crazy."

"What were you doing outside?"

He shrugged. "Walking. On the beach. I had some thinking to do."

"About…?"

"Us." He sighed. His frustration was palpable. "Us" had no easy answer. "Us" wasn't something that could be settled in one long walk on the beach.

His gaze swept down her body to where he still held the cloth. He removed it and dabbed her gently with the dry towel, then rolled up the wet cloth in it and dropped it on the floor. She tugged his T-shirt up. He helped pull it over his head even as his eyes questioned her.

She said, "Stay with me tonight," and unzipped his jeans.

By the time he had the rest of his clothes off, his erection had returned with a vengeance. He drew the covers over them and reached for the light switch. She stayed his hand.

"Not so fast," she said.

His chuckle was a little strained. "Honey, you're in no shape for a return engagement." He glanced at the tent he'd pitched in the bedcovers. "Much as we wish you were."

"And I always thought you had such a healthy imagination."

His eyes flashed to hers, and what she saw there made her insides clench. Yes, he could still do it to her.

With just a look.

He shifted onto his side, facing her, smiling silkily. "Nothing wrong with my imagination."

"So glad to hear it." She let her hand drift under the covers to close around his rigid penis. He sucked in a breath. Holding his gaze, she slid her fingers from tip to base and lower, to cup the potent heaviness there. She stroked him slowly, leisurely, reacquainting herself with his contours, the hot velvet smoothness of him. He twitched impatiently under her fingers.

Just the thought of this part of him deep inside her, of this man joined so intimately with her, took her breath away. She edged closer until his erection brushed her belly. He let out a pent-up breath and moved against her.

She pushed him onto his back, and he let her. His chest rose and fell faster, his intense gaze tracking her every move. Never had he looked so flagrantly, so unapologetically male. She pulled the covers down to bare him to her.

"I've missed you," she whispered, bending to press kisses to his chest, trailing her breasts across his hair-roughened torso. The scent of their lovemaking lingered, an aphrodisiac.

He swallowed hard and ran trembling hands over her hair, her shoulders. She sensed his leashed power, the obvious effort he exerted to keep from throwing her on her back and taking her again with the same mindless fervor as before.

The tip of her tongue lazily circled his nipple, wringing a guttural sigh from him. Her teeth nipped him lightly, followed by broad, healing licks. Something akin to a warning growl rumbled deep in his chest. She smiled.

Sliding down his body, she let her stiff nipple graze his erection, which leaped in response. She caressed him with her breasts, moving sinuously, delighting in his writhing, coiling hunger.

Abruptly his fingers slid into her hair and splayed over her scalp. Desire pulsed hard within her as he steered her lips to his penis. Eagerly she kissed a path to the glistening tip and took him in her mouth. A strangled gasp escaped him. Every muscle in his body tensed; his fingers tightened on her scalp as he guided her movements.

After a minute she rose up and straddled him. If this was to be their only time together, she couldn't let him go without taking him inside her once more. He seized her hips, holding her just above his straining erection.

"Meg, don't. You're already tender." His voice was hoarse. A hint of a smile touched his eyes. "Your turn's next, honey. I won't let you down."

She knew what he meant. He intended to pleasure her the same way she'd been pleasuring him. A tempting offer, but...

"It's not enough," she said. "I want you. I need you.

Inside me." She rubbed the blunt tip of him against herself, teasing them both.

She saw the instant his resistance snapped. He eased his hold on her hips, his eyes burning into hers. She lowered herself slowly, and slower still as her body protested. Half-impaled, she stopped altogether. Helpless laughter overtook her, and infected him.

He asked, "Why are we laughing?"

"Damned if I know. I'm *so sore!*"

For some reason, that made them laugh harder. "Honey," he said with a chuckle, "come on, let's be sensible about this." But he made no move to withdraw from her.

Biting her lip to quell her giggles, she continued her slow progress, taking him in inch by inch until he was finally buried to the hilt. She rested a moment.

He shook his head, smirking. "This one's not my doing. If you end up hobbling around tomorrow, I don't want to hear about regrets."

Speaking of which... "You know, we didn't use birth control," she said.

"Oh damn! I didn't pack any—"

He cut off the last word, but it ricocheted around in her head anyway, like some deranged pinball.

Condoms.

She and Jack had never used birth control during their marriage. Nevertheless, it was painfully obvious that what he'd failed to pack in his duffel he had in plentiful supply back home, probably in his night-table drawer.

So he'd purchased them. And used them. So what?

Jack was too smart to practice unsafe sex. She wouldn't think about him with those other women. Not now. She'd lost enough sleep last night doing just that, and she no doubt would again.

But not here. Not now. This was their precious time together, and it belonged to them alone.

She said, "Well, it's a little late to think about birth control now. What's that expression?" Tentatively she moved her hips, gratified to find that pleasure had triumphed over pain. "No sense closing the barn door...?"

"After the horse has escaped." His smile was pure bliss as she lowered herself on him once more.

"Too late to lasso the sucker now," she added. "What are you doing?"

He was rolling them onto their sides, facing each other, still joined. "This might be a little easier on you." He pulled her top leg over his, curled his long arms around her and began thrusting cautiously, letting her set the pace.

"Oh yes," she said with a sigh. "Oh, Jack, that's..." And then speech failed her; she could only moan. The rhythmic pressure of his hard thigh between hers amplified her pleasure.

Lifting her breast, he bent his head and sucked the tip into his hot mouth. She gasped as a spike of lightning streaked from that point straight down to where they were connected. And still they moved with infinite slowness, melding, retreating. She pushed her fingers into his wavy hair, holding him to her.

Closing her eyes, she let the raw carnality of it cascade over her, through her—the voluptuous tug of his mouth on her breast, the languid ebb and flow of their lower bodies. It was too pure, too achingly sweet.

He released her breast and pressed his palm to the sensitized tip. "You're smiling."

Her eyes drifted open and her smile grew broader as she felt the wispy threads of her orgasm begin to gather. It was distant yet unavoidable, a thunderstorm brewing somewhere in the vicinity of New Jersey. And still they rocked together, slow as molasses.

How had she lived two years without this?

Jack's eyes crinkled as he watched her. She couldn't hide the signs of her impending climax if she'd wanted to. Her urgent sighs. Her greedy, clutching hands. Her dopey, preorgasmic expression.

As if he'd read her mind, he murmured, "You're beautiful like this. Right before. So beautiful." His fingers lightly traced her face, lingered on her flared nostrils, her parted lips. He shifted a little and his thigh pressed harder, right there. She groaned, the sound prolonged and shockingly erotic to her ears.

He was pacing her, she could tell, holding off his own release, waiting for her to catch up. And still they maintained the same sluggish tempo, honing anticipation to an exquisitely keen edge, in defiance of every instinct screaming, *Faster!*

In the next instant, a blinding orgasm had her in its teeth. She bucked into him hard at the first shock wave. Grinning, Jack drawled, "Oh yeah..." and let himself go.

Meg forced her eyes open to watch his face as he

came, awed yet again by the pure masculine vitality and beauty of this man who'd never stopped loving her.

It seemed to go on forever, in pulsating bursts. At last they lay in a boneless jumble of entwined limbs, twitching from the aftershocks. After several minutes their breathing quieted and their heartbeats slowed.

Her eyes closed, Meg whispered, "I love you, Jack. I always have."

He stroked her brow; she felt the tension there, and realized she was frowning.

He said, "I wish you could smile when you say that. I wish your love for me were a joyous thing. It once was, you know. At one time I made you happy."

I could again. If you let me. He didn't say it. He didn't have to.

He added, "I've never stopped loving you."

Tears burned behind her closed eyelids and leaked out the corners. His rough fingertips captured them.

"Don't, Meg. Don't cry, honey. I'm not worth crying over."

Her eyes snapped open. She shoved at his chest. "Don't say that. I've shed gallons of tears over you, you bastard. Don't you dare tell me you're not worth it!"

He opened his mouth and shut it. His breath escaped in a long, flummoxed sigh.

They stared at each other in the soft lamplight. Jack studied her intently, as if trying to read her innermost thoughts. *Good luck.* They were illegible even to her.

Finally he said, "You're rattled right now. You've

got a right to be. Hell, with what you've had to deal with the last few days, you should be a gibbering nutcase by now. But I want you to understand something." He leaned up on an elbow. "When this craziness is all over, when the dust settles, I'll be waiting. If you think I'm going to just slink back out of your life and let you pretend we don't love each other and belong together, think again. I made it too easy for you to do that once. It's not going to happen a second time. Not without a fight.

"And before you get any ideas, this has nothing to do with Pete's money," he added. "You were dirt-poor when I fell in love with you. I've wanted you back since the day you left me, and I'd want you even if you didn't have a pot to—"

"I know it's not the money." She couldn't help but smile at the vehemence of his declaration. And at the ludicrous picture he painted. Jack Wolf, a gigolo? Between his fierce entrepreneurial spirit and his innate sense of honor, that was one thing he could never be. She said, "I know you just want me for the sex."

His lips quirked. "As long as we're clear on that." He reached behind him to switch off the lamp, then pulled the covers up and snuggled her against him.

10

"SAUSAGE?" Jack speared a greasy link on a fork and thrust it under Winston's nose.

Pillowy, bloodshot eyes focused on the thing for the barest instant before Winston averted his face. "No," he rasped. "Thank you." His complexion was gray, his hair matted.

"Eggs, then." Jack lifted a platter from the dining room table and slid the last of the fried eggs onto Winston's plate—three jiggly sunny-side-ups. The whites were runny, just the way he'd taught the girls to like them.

Winston reared back and shoved the plate away with his good hand. His throat worked and sweat beaded on his upper lip. He appeared to be approaching critical mass. The guy may have spent yesterday guzzling fifty-dollar single-malt Scotch, but Jack knew a Mad Dog hangover when he saw one.

"Mr. Kent has a headache, Daddy." Marie dunked a strip of toast in her yolk and bit off a chunk. From Winston's expression, he might have been watching a crow gorging on roadkill. Starting with the eyes.

Nora asked, "Does your belly hurt, too, Mr. Kent?"

"Immeasurably."

She frowned.

"That means yes," Jack said.

"Here. You can have my oatmeal." She slid a steaming, mucilaginous bowlful in front of him. "Oatmeal's good when you got a bellyache."

Marie said, "Once I had a virus and I didn't want to throw up, and Mommy said when I threw up I'd feel better, so I did, I threw up, and I *did* feel better. Maybe you just need to throw up, Mr. Kent."

Daisy parroted, "Fwow up, Mr. Kent," and slurped a gelatinous gob of egg white off her fork.

The sound of Winston's chair scraping the floor was drowned out by Meg's jovial "I'm starved!" She beamed at them from the doorway of the dining room, her gaze quickly sliding away from her erstwhile fiancé. "I could eat a horse! Do I smell sausage? I *love* sausage!" Slowly she made her way to the chair across from Jack's, her gait stiff-legged but stately, as if walking were a skill she'd only recently mastered.

Watching her, Jack was reminded of that old joke in which the Norse god of thunder reveals his true identity to his mortal lover after a godlike marathon lovemaking session. She lisps, "*You're* thor? *I'm* tho thor I can hardly—*"

Winston's head whipped back around and he harpooned Jack with a look of bug-eyed outrage.

He knew.

Jack stared him down for several long, triumphant seconds, his expression outwardly neutral. This was the look that he imagined had passed from Ulysses S. Grant to Robert E. Lee at Appomattox. Only he and Winston were privy to this silent communiqué, the females in the room being biologically unequipped to decipher the subtle male message.

I won, you lost, nyah nyah nyah.

Winston's features were rigid. "Excuse me. I find I can no longer stomach even the thought of breakfast." He rose and pushed in his chair, obviously struggling to salvage some dignity.

Meg gingerly lowered her bottom to her chair, eyeing the eggs on Winston's plate. "You're not going to eat those?"

"No, but do feel free. Nothing would give me greater pleasure than to satisfy your *prodigious* appetite."

"Great!" She scooped the eggs onto her plate, followed by mounds of sausage and toast.

Jack smiled. Good sex had always made Meg hungry as a half-starved linebacker. It was a wonder her slender figure had survived their passionate marriage. Of course, there was always the possibility she was eating for two now; they were a ridiculously fertile couple. He berated himself for his lack of caution. He'd been so conscientious since the divorce, never once taking a chance, and here he'd failed to protect the one woman who'd ever meant anything to him.

When Winston disappeared through the doorway, Meg sent Jack a lopsided smile. "Feeling poorly, is he?"

"Probably wishes he'd stuck to aspirin."

Marie and Nora announced they were finished. Jack reminded them to carry their plates into the kitchen, and they grumblingly complied. Daisy jumped up to follow them. Meg corralled her and managed to swab her face and hands with napkins while the child squirmed impatiently.

Jack said, "Speaking of feeling poorly..." and let a suggestive smile say the rest.

She colored becomingly. "I don't know what you mean. I feel fine." She removed the egg-splotched napkin that had been tucked into the collar of Daisy's shirt and sent her on her way with a pat to her little rump.

He poured Meg a cup of coffee. "Didn't I warn you you'd be hobbling around?"

"I'm not hobbling! I'm walking completely naturally. Kind of."

"Want me to kiss it all better?"

"Jack!" Her gaze flew to the open doorway.

"It'd be no trouble. Really."

"We have more important things to talk about," she said, digging into her eggs.

"What's more important than sex?"

"Murder."

Now *his* eyes went to the doorway. He lowered his voice and leaned across the table. "What's on your mind?"

"That boat's going to come for us in—" she checked her watch "—three hours, more or less. We'll get the captain to call the police on his radio, and then we'll have to wait for the police boat and answer all sorts of questions and who knows what all."

He grimaced. "We *might* get away from this island sometime today."

Now she leaned across the table. "We should plan what we're going to tell the police."

"About what?"

She glanced at the doorway once more. "Our suspicions. If someone in this house murdered my uncle, I don't want them getting away with it!"

"Do you think I do? Look, it's no secret I hated the son of a bitch, but that's beside the point."

"Either one of us can be made to look guilty as sin. Did you think of that?"

"I've thought of it," he said grimly. He wasn't concerned for himself—he'd endured worse. But the thought of Meg being questioned as a suspect gnawed at his gut.

She said, "You threatened him in front of witnesses, and I stand to inherit a fortune. Whoever really is guilty wouldn't hesitate to point the finger at one or both of us."

"So you want to get the jump on him."

"Or her. Any more thoughts on who the culprit is?"

"Too many. Our housemates aren't exactly Donny and Marie Osmond. One thing, though, keeps coming back to me."

"What's that?" She polished off a slice of toast and started in on the sausage.

"Something Tanya said. Friday night after you went out for your walk. She said something like not to worry, she'd taken care of things. 'Taken steps,' was how she put it."

"Could be she meant she'd placed a big order with a sex-toy catalog."

"Things would work out, she said. I had no idea what she meant. Still don't."

Meg lifted her coffee cup. "Maybe it's time to find out." She wagged her eyebrows, the message clear. He was to use his masculine wiles to extract information from their hostess.

Jack shuddered dramatically.

Meg's eyes twinkled—they actually *twinkled*, the witch! "You can do it, big fella. Just don't let her find that knockwurst."

JACK HAD TO WAIT nearly two more hours for Bonnie and Clyde to roll out of bed. He was beginning to worry that the charter boat would show up before he had a chance to get Tanya alone for a cozy little chat.

Neal slimed out of her room first, scratching his armpit and asking if the phone was still out. He didn't seem to notice that no one bothered to answer him. Tanya made an appearance about twenty minutes later, after troweling on her makeup and teasing her hair. Her pneumatic lushness had been poured into a low-cut, shiny gold sweater and tight purple leggings tucked into high-heeled black boots.

Jack intercepted her at the bottom of the stairs. Making an elaborate show of ensuring he wasn't overheard, he murmured, "I think it's time we had that little talk."

Her sleep-puffy eyes widened. She smiled. "Lemme grab a cup of coffee first."

He put a restraining hand on her arm. "I said *now*." This little exhibition of manly boorishness had the desired effect. She seemed to melt around the edges, like a Hershey's Bar left out in the sun. He said, "Get your jacket."

Her face fell. "It's *cold* out there!"

"Get your jacket." With a meaningful glance, he added, "There's no privacy in the house."

A slow smile curved her lips. "It's not *that* cold."

Outside, it was not only cold, but overcast as well. A bitter dampness heralded rain. He hoped it would hold off at least until the police had finished their work here. Tanya hugged her sable jacket close to her body and tottered across the lawn in Jack's wake.

"We're not going in *there*, are we?" She pointed toward the distant boathouse, now serving as a temporary morgue, her scowl revealing equal parts trepidation and disgust.

He'd enjoy that, he thought with a grim smile. Locking Tanya Stanton in that little building with her dead husband and presumptive murder victim. The idea had a Poe-like elegance. *Tales from the Boathouse.*

"Don't worry," he said, and led her behind the toolshed, where they were out of the wind. She catapulted herself at him, but he was ready. His hands shot out to keep her at arm's length.

He said, "Let's get something straight right now. *I'm* the man here. You want to call the shots, go back to that little boy you've been wearing out." He jerked his head toward the house.

"But I've waited *so long* for you!" she wailed, her breath smoking.

"And you'll keep on waiting. You'll wait until I decide you're good and ready for it." Recalling her words from the night she'd jumped him on the sofa, he added, "No woman tells me what to do. Or when to do it. You got that?"

She nodded. The gesture was meek, but the look in her eyes was downright gluttonous.

"First," he said, "we've got to compare notes—before the cops show up."

"Why? We both know what's what. You did your part and I did mine. Now we just sit back and let the pieces fall into place."

Her words brought to mind something else she'd said Friday night—that he was a man of action and had proved it. The implications made his flesh crawl. He said, "Meg's going to tell the cops someone planted the ring and will in her luggage."

"Of course she will. Wouldn't any guilty person say that? I'm sure the cops'll think so. Why do we have to hash all this out? I'm cold. I need someone to warm me up." She pouted, a look she might have gotten away with when she was sixteen. Now it just made her look pathetic and worn-out.

She added, "Look, don't worry about anyone believing Meg. Even her fiancé thinks she's guilty."

"*Former* fiancé."

Tanya's eyes shot to his. He'd made a tactical error. "You *do* want her back," she accused.

"Yeah, right. That's just what I need, that shrew back in my life to nag me into an early grave."

She preened. "Some women just can't appreciate a

man who's...masterful. Lucky for you, I'm not one of those women."

Yeah, lucky me.

He said, "So to get back to the ring and the will..." Might as well jump in with both feet. She sure wasn't going to make it easy for him. "When did you put them in her room?"

She stared at him for a minute, her lips compressed, her expression unreadable. Could his instincts be wrong? Had Neal planted that evidence in Meg's luggage?

Then there was Winston. Jack hadn't seriously considered him a suspect, but was it possible...?

She said, "You're just not gonna let this rest, are you? Why do we have to talk about it?"

"'Cause it gets me hot."

Now he had her attention.

He said, "It excites me, thinking about what you've been up to behind everyone's backs. A regular Mata Hari." He leaned a shoulder against the wall of the toolshed, his hands stuffed in his jacket pockets. He eyed her up and down. "I want to hear it from you. Every detail. Don't leave anything out."

Her eyes glittered. "Where should I start?"

"At the beginning. Thanksgiving night. What happened after you and Neal left me in the living room and went into the den?"

"Well, first I put my tongue in his ear—"

"Not those details. What did you do after?"

"We went to bed. Our own beds," she amended. "Only, when I was sneaking back into my room, I saw something funny at the end of the hall—I couldn't tell what. Neal had the flashlight, so I slipped into my room for a candle, and that's when I saw Pete wasn't in bed. He was asleep when I left him earlier. Anyway, I had this funny feeling when I went back out with the candle. I guess I wasn't surprised when I found him there. At the bottom of the steps."

"He was already dead."

"Sure."

If she was telling the truth, Neal could still be guilty. *If* he could have managed to wake his father, get him into the attic and slam him down the stairs while Tanya was trying to seduce Jack on the sofa right below. Not a very promising window of opportunity.

"So you found him first," Jack said.

She nodded.

"And you didn't do anything."

"Do anything?"

"You didn't wake anybody up, sound the alarm. You know."

"If I did that, everyone would've known I took it."

"The ring."

"Of course, the ring. I figured why should I share with Neal?"

He straightened. "Then you already knew about the revised will."

"Well, duh. Pete went to his lawyer's a couple of weeks ago, and it didn't take a genius to figure out why. I thought we were being, you know, discreet, me and Neal, but I guess Pete just had a dirty mind." She shrugged. "Anyway, a little snooping around turned up the new will. I made a copy."

"Which you stashed in Meg's luggage, along with the ring. When? Friday?"

"Yep. While you and Winston were out chopping wood and Meg was taking a bath with Daisy. Neal was watching football in the den. Are you hot yet?"

"Gettin' there. Why did you part with the ring? It's worth thousands."

She said, "You know why. Did you really think I'd let you go back to jail? After what you did to have me?"

He tried not to let his sudden comprehension—and revulsion—show on his face.

She sidled up to him and slid her hands up his jacket. "You killed for me," she purred. "You saw your opportunity and you took it. You did what you had to do so you and me could be together. And I did what I had to do to keep you from getting caught—I made it look like Meg did it."

Her hands started to slip around his neck. He caught her wrists and set her away from him, less than gently, choking on his anger. "Why Meg?" he asked. "Why not Neal? Or Winston?"

"The money, of course. You couldn't have known he cut me out of his will, but I did. And I knew if Meg went to jail for Pete's murder, they'd never let her collect that inheritance. I'm betting it'll all go to me. Even if I have to share it with Neal, it's still a helluva sweeter deal than half of that ring."

Jack suspected Tanya's motives for incriminating

Meg went beyond simple greed. She was eliminating the competition. After all, with his ex-wife behind bars, there'd be even less chance of a reconciliation. He thought of the repercussions if this woman's demented plan were to succeed: his three little girls torn from their mother, growing up knowing she'd been convicted of murder.

Struggling to control his temper, he spun away from Tanya just in time to see a large shape hurling itself at him.

He went down with a grunt even as his well-honed reflexes kicked in. Neal was surprisingly strong and youthfully quick despite his affection for bourbon. He lashed out with everything he had, and it took everything Jack had to fend him off. A wild jab caught Jack in the mouth. Meanwhile Tanya stood shrieking at her stepson.

In a few swift moves Jack had him pinned facedown. Still the young man struggled, his face purple with rage.

"Give it up, Neal," Jack said, and spit blood onto the ground. "You're not gonna win this one."

"You killed my dad! I heard it all, you son of a bitch. You killed him! Just so you could have his money, and that whore he married!"

Tanya screeched, "What?"

He must have been listening on the other side of the shed. "I didn't kill him," Jack said. "That's your stepmother's version of events. And if you were listening long enough, you know Meg's innocent, too. Now, settle down!"

Tentatively he loosened his grip and backed off. Neal leaped up, glaring at them with undisguised loathing. "You two had it all worked out, didn't you? Bump off the old man and share everything he worked so hard for."

He stood quivering with outrage over his father's death. He couldn't have faked the pain Jack saw in his eyes. The bond of blood held strong, despite the strained relationship between father and son, the betrayal and animosity. Neal's grief was the real McCoy, not the playacting of a murderer.

Tanya planted her hands on her hips and glowered at Neal. "Did you call me a *whore?*"

The two men ignored her. Neal said, "You're pitiful, Wolf, a stupid, bumbling ex-con who thinks he can get away with murder. Everyone heard you threaten him. You had motive, opportunity, the works. When the cops get here, it'll be all over. I'm gonna enjoy watching you leave this island on a police boat, in handcuffs."

11

"NEAL HASN'T CHANGED MUCH," Meg observed, gently dabbing at the bruised and swollen corner of Jack's mouth with a damp cloth. "Still flies off the handle like a little kid."

From his perch on a kitchen bar stool, Jack watched her eyes as she ministered to him, soaking up the loving concern he saw there. As for Neal, no angel of mercy lavished attention on him. He sat in solitary misery in the den, sucking down liquid therapy while a lovely shiner blossomed on his eye.

Neal's spiteful words drew a gut-churning picture in Jack's head. *I'm gonna enjoy watching you leave this island on a police boat, in handcuffs.* When Jack had left prison so long ago, he'd made a vow to himself never to return. He'd spent the intervening years remaking his life, building a business and a family. How could he have predicted that accepting a last-minute invitation to spend a holiday with Meg's relatives would jeopardize everything he'd struggled so hard for? He imagined Pete Stanton, pitchfork in hand, peering up at him through layers of bedrock and laughing himself silly.

Neal was right about how it looked, how the police would see it. Jack was an ex-con who'd threatened the deceased in front of witnesses. Motive, opportunity, means were all there—it would have made a lively round of Murder Won.

Even if Pete had fallen down the stairs with no assistance and that bat wasn't involved—which was looking more likely by the minute—it could still be made to look like Jack pushed him. Contrary to what he'd told Meg, he had been in the attic, after all; his fingerprints were all over the place. And he had no doubt Tanya would point the finger at him. A woman scorned and all that. But God help anyone who tried to implicate Meg.

Meg's brow knit. "So Neal didn't kill him. And it looks like it wasn't Tanya, either, since she's so certain you did it. You don't think..." She cast her eyes to the ceiling, and the bedroom where Winston was trying to sleep off his hangover.

"Do you think he could've done it?" he asked.

"I didn't before, but now I'm not so sure. What with the other two suddenly looking pure as the driven snow."

They shared a smirk over that notion. Jack said, "I don't think Winston could've done it. For one thing, I literally don't think he could've done it. He's a self-important jerk, but come on—he's no killer. For another thing, if he'd gone to all the trouble of sniffing out the revised will and icing your uncle so he could marry a wealthy woman, the last thing he'd do is stand there and mouth off about how guilty you looked, I don't care how sozzled he was. He'd have been turning on the charm, doing everything he could to keep you."

Meg grimaced. "He didn't exactly put up a fight when I broke off the engagement. I think he really believes I'm a murderer, Jack."

Her voice wobbled. She hurt, and he hurt for her. She'd committed herself to Winston, placed her future in his hands. Jack now knew she'd never really loved the guy, but she'd trusted and respected him. And what did he do but turn on her when she most needed his support and faith.

She said, "He was acting strange even before that stuff turned up in my luggage. Hectoring me about my thighs and my language and all. What was that about, do you think?"

Jack shrugged, all innocence, but she knew him too well. "What?" she demanded. "What did you do?"

"I'm injured. Don't yell at me."

Her eyes narrowed. "What did you say to Winston?"

"I, uh, might've explained how much you value constructive criticism."

"Constructive criticism."

He grinned with all the boyish charm at his disposal.

She wasn't impressed. "You're shameless."

"This is news?"

"To get back to the subject at hand," she said. "It wasn't Tanya, Neal or Winston. We're agreed on that. And it wasn't you or me."

"I've got it!"

Meg looked at him expectantly.

"It was Marie!" he declared. "I knew we shouldn't have enrolled her in Little League. You've seen her with a bat—kid's got a helluva swing."

Meg snorted and slapped his arm playfully. "I can't believe you have me laughing about a thing like that. We're terrible."

"We're coping. There's a difference." He pulled her close to the bar stool and trapped her between his legs. Cupping her face in his hands, he placed a soft kiss on her lips. "Ow," he murmured against her mouth, his own smarting from its encounter with Neal's fist.

She smiled. "Love hurts."

He pulled back. "Are the kids still up in their room?"

She nodded. "They're constructing the most intricate model railroad you've ever seen. I was about to call them down for an early lunch."

"Let them play. It's time for a house meeting."

"IS THAT WHY YOU CALLED us in here?" Winston grumbled. "To tell us we're all innocent?"

Jack had just laid it all out, methodically eliminating suspects in the murder of Pete Stanton, the man everyone wanted dead.

Wincing, Neal slumped lower in his father's favorite easy chair, glaring at Jack out of the eye that wasn't swollen shut. "Why should we believe you didn't do it, Wolf? 'Cause you say so? That'll really cut a lot of ice with the cops."

Tanya sat on the sofa, blessedly silent for once, arms

and legs firmly crossed. She looked sulky and haggard, and Jack knew why. Not only had he not killed for her, he'd tricked her into spilling her guts. Now everyone knew about the ring and the will and her attempt to frame Meg.

"I don't care whether you believe me or not," Jack said. "I just don't want the police showing up with things still in an uproar, us accusing each other, with no answers to the most obvious questions."

Meg said, "The most obvious being—"

Everyone else chimed in tiredly: "Why was Pete in the attic?"

She added, "It would appear that he died of natural causes—had some kind of spell that made him fall down the stairs. Tanya, did he have any medical conditions? Weak heart, anything?"

"I don't know! What do I look like, his mother?"

Winston straightened. "I'll tell you the obvious question to which I'd like an answer. Why did our friend here—" with his good hand he gestured toward Jack "—refuse to let us search his luggage? Odd behavior for a man with nothing to hide."

Yesterday Winston had seemed convinced of Jack's innocence, or at least willing to extend the benefit of the doubt. But of course, that was before he'd spent the night with the man's almost-fiancée.

Everyone looked at Jack, awaiting his response. Everyone except Meg.

"Jack had nothing to do with Pete's death," she declared, passionate color infusing her face. She'd never looked more beautiful. "We all know Tanya was behind that stupid search. She manipulated us into going along with it for her own self-serving purposes. Maybe Jack just had it all figured out and refused to participate in that sham."

He loved her for standing up for him, but he couldn't take the easy out she was offering. He'd seen her face when he'd refused the search. There was only one thing to do. Get it over with.

"Better late than never," he said, striding to the corner where his duffel lay. He hauled it into the center of the room and unzipped it.

Meg said, "Jack, that's not neces—"

"Yes it is. And besides..." He smiled grimly as he pulled his clothing out of the bag to expose what lay at the bottom. "The cops'll take a look anyway, so what the hell."

"A photo album?" Tanya said when he revealed his ill-gotten gains.

He laid the old album on the coffee table. Its cloth cover was frayed at the edges.

Meg said, "Jack...I don't understand. This is what you didn't want anyone to find?"

He made himself look her in the eye. "I came across it in the attic when I first got here on Thursday, before you arrived. I'd gone up there to see if I could find any old toys for the kids."

She blinked. "You told me you'd never been in the attic." She flipped to the middle of the album and saw a snapshot of herself at about age ten, building a sand castle on the beach. Most of the other pictures were of her as well, from infancy to adolescence. She'd always been Pete's favorite niece.

"I didn't want you to find out I'd made off with this," he said. "I figured if I couldn't have you, at least I could have these pictures. I was embarrassed, giving in to that kind of mawkish sentimentality. Pretty pathetic, huh?"

Tanya apparently thought so. "Oh brother."

Jack ignored her, and the rest of them. Meg was the only one who mattered, after all.

Neal said, "What else have you swiped from my dead father, Wolf?"

Jack never took his eyes from Meg. "I told you the other night I haven't done anything illegal since I walked out of prison sixteen years ago. This was the one exception. God knows if I'd asked Pete for it, he would've laughed in my face."

She picked up the album and replaced it in his duffel. "Well, it's my property now, so consider it a gift."

Winston's tone was arid. "I can't tell you how moving this has been. Now we know what Jack was doing in the attic, but the quandary still remains—what compelled Pete to venture up there in the middle of the night?"

Meg said, "Did anyone check his pockets before you moved him?"

The men looked at one another. Jack said, "He was wearing a robe over pajamas. I didn't see any pockets."

She said, "He showed me that robe when he got it from Hong Kong. He was very proud of it. It was custom-made to his specifications. There are two deep pockets set into the side seams. You might not have noticed them."

Neal added, "Especially with the old man's gut in the way."

In the silence that followed, Jack could almost hear the synapses snapping in their collective gray matter. The same thought had to be occurring to all of them. Finally Tanya expressed it in her own inimitable way.

"Eww...you aren't going to start digging through his pockets, are you?"

"No, you are," Jack said.

"*What?*"

"Just kidding. Don't worry, I'll do it."

Neal sat up straighter. "No you don't. I don't trust you."

Jack shrugged. "So come with me."

"Let the police look through his pockets, all that stuff," Neal said. "You do it and you're messing with a criminal investigation."

Winston said, "It's beginning to look as if no crime has been committed. I think the rest of us are in agreement about that, even if you aren't, Neal. I agree with Jack. If we wait for the police to take action, they're certain to treat this as a criminal investigation, at least initially. Which would be vastly inconvenient for all concerned. Whereas if we're able to present them with concrete answers to those bothersome questions up front, we might save ourselves a great deal of time and trouble in the long run. Am I making sense?"

"You are indeed, Counselor," Jack said, impressed

by this fair-minded assessment from a man who had every right to hate his guts. If would have been easy for Winston to take Neal's side just to make things rough for Jack.

He met Winston's gaze briefly and was reminded of their conversation by the woodpile, when he'd decided the man wasn't the one-dimensional joke he'd originally thought. A wordless communication passed between them now, a kind of grudging respect that went both ways.

Meg said, "I say we all go out there."

"No, thanks!" Tanya said. "I'll stay here and baby-sit."

Winston said, "There's absolutely no reason to subject the ladies to—"

"Winston." Meg held up a hand. "I appreciate the gallant gesture, but it's okay. Really."

Jack said, "Meg—"

"For heaven's sake, Jack! I won't faint."

And she didn't, but only through an effort of will. She stood in the doorway of the boathouse, taking deep, slow breaths, as the men peeled the tarp from Uncle Pete's body, which lay on the wooden floor. She was shaking so badly she expected her legs to give out any moment.

"What d'ya know," Jack said, squatting by the body, poking at the side seams of Pete's voluminous robe. "Pockets." He checked the left-hand one and came up empty. Stepping over the body, he slipped his hand in the right-hand pocket.

"Come on," Neal said, his breath fogging. "This place gives me the—"

The look on Jack's face brought instant silence. He slowly withdrew his hand and displayed his find.

A tiny pistol—bright nickel with a wooden stock. It literally fit in the palm of his hand.

"Oh my God," Meg breathed.

Winston seconded this with "My word!"

Neal let out a long, low whistle.

Jack examined the gun. "It's a Baretta, .25 caliber. Not too powerful, but deadly enough at close range." He pointed it at the floor and ejected the magazine. "It's loaded—" he pulled back the slide and peered into it "—and there's a round in the chamber."

"What does that mean?" Meg's voice quavered. She wrapped her arms around her middle, fighting a sick wave of dread.

Winston answered, his expression somber. "It means Pete had cocked the gun. He was preparing to use it."

Neal made a grab for the pistol, but Jack was faster. Neal snarled, "You're not keeping that thing!"

"It belongs to Meg now," Jack calmly said. "Meg?"

She lifted her palms. "I'd like you to hold on to it for now."

Jack unloaded the gun and pocketed it and the bullets.

Winston asked, "How on earth did we miss that thing when we moved him?"

"Well, that silk is thickly quilted," Meg said, "and

so is Uncle Pete. A tiny gun like that in a hidden pocket? I'm not surprised you didn't find it."

"Let's see if Pete had any more surprises for us." Jack slid his hand into the robe pocket once more. "No... Yes!" He held up a tiny brass key. "Almost missed it. Neal, any idea what this opens?"

"No."

"And if you knew, you wouldn't tell me, right?"

A surly silence was his only answer. The men folded the tarp back over Pete. They filed out and locked the boathouse, then started trudging back to the house.

Winston said, "I haven't been in the attic. Is anything up there under lock and key?"

The same thought had to have occurred to Jack. Meg met his eyes and knew it had.

"There's a safe," Jack said. "An old wall safe. It opens with a key rather than a combination."

"Well," Winston said. "I suppose I needn't ask what our next stop is."

Their hostess joined them on their sojourn into the attic. They watched as Jack inserted the key in the lock of the safe. It fit perfectly. The heavy steel door swung open with a squeal of rusty hinges.

A smell emerged from the interior, a pungent, almost sweet scent that Meg didn't recognize. But Jack apparently did. And Winston, as well. They exchanged a look.

"Hoppe's," Jack said, as he withdrew a greasy rag from the safe and sniffed it.

Meg asked, "What's that?"

"Gun cleaner. The pistol must've been wrapped in this cloth. And..." He pulled a small box out of the safe. "Bullets, .25 caliber."

"That's what Pete went up here for in the middle of the night?" Tanya asked. "His gun?" She was looking a little peaked under her Max Factor.

"Looks that way," Jack said.

"From what you told us, there was a bit of activity just before Pete died," Winston reminded them.

"The place was hopping. I'd just chased these two out of the living room so I could get some sleep," Jack said, nodding toward Neal and Tanya.

"I don't remember it like that," Neal said.

Tanya muttered, "I do."

Winston continued, "Meg, you said you heard Pete fall down the stairs about 1:00 a.m."

"I think I did." She bit her lip, recalling her nightmare and the thudding sound that grew louder and stopped abruptly. "I'm pretty sure I did, yeah."

No one spoke for a minute, as an ugly scenario presented itself. In her mind's eye Meg saw Uncle Pete slipping up here on Thanksgiving night, in the grip of a killing rage...opening his safe, loading his gun....

Finally Winston said quietly, "I wish I could say I'm surprised."

Tanya said, "You don't really think...Pete wasn't going to..."

"He heard us," Neal said, his face pinched in anguish. "He heard us arguing, me and Jack and Tanya. He knew what we'd been doing right under his nose.

And he came up here for his gun." His voice cracked at the end.

Tanya shuddered, her eyes wide. She whispered, "Who was he gonna shoot?"

"My guess?" Jack said. "All three of us."

"No." Tanya shook her head. "Not me. He loved me. He would never..."

"There's something else in here," Jack said, reaching into the safe. He extracted a large brown envelope and slid out the contents, a sheaf of eight-by-ten black-and-white photos. Everyone crowded around to look.

After a moment of stunned silence Tanya shrieked and lunged for the photos. Jack held them out of reach.

"My word!" Winston scrutinized the top picture closely. "I never knew one could do that with a soap on a rope. Who's that young fellow with you?"

"His name is Benny," Tanya answered through clenched teeth. "He delivers pizzas for Mario's."

Neal grabbed the top few pictures and shuffled through them quickly, his face mottled. "What'd you do, Tanya, work your way along the North Shore?" He wagged a photo in her face. "Starting with the high school football team?"

"I don't get this one." Jack turned a picture sideways. "Oh yeah, now I do. Looks like you're getting some very private lessons from your tennis coach."

A dark flush crawled up Tanya's throat. "I was having trouble with my backswing."

"I'd say you have the problem licked." He came to the next shot. "Ah, there you are, Neal."

Winston peered over Jack's shoulder and winced. "Doesn't that smart?"

Neal could only stare in mute shock at the evidence of his perfidy, there in glossy black and white for the world to see. Meg backed away. She didn't even want to know.

Tanya wailed, "I can't believe that fat old slob hired someone to follow me around and take pictures!"

Jack straightened the stack of photos and slid them into the envelope. "No doubt the same PI he sicced on me. Guy knows his stuff, I'll give him that."

Meg said, "I don't think there's any question what Uncle Pete had in mind when he came up here. Something happened to him, though, to keep him from following through."

Winston looked at the stairway Pete had tumbled down. "He had to have been in a highly emotional state, a blind homicidal fury. I'd guess it triggered a heart attack, perhaps a stroke..."

Thank God, Meg silently added, stunned by the turn of events, by the appalling fact that she felt grateful for her uncle's sudden death. If Pete's body hadn't failed him at that critical moment, more than one person would have been leaving this island in a body bag. Including Jack.

My God, she thought, *I almost lost Jack!* Her mind rebelled, the thought too horrific, too crushing, to contemplate. She'd lost her husband once, but if Pete had had his way, there would have been no turning back, no second chance.

Second chance.

If two sweeter words existed, she didn't know what they were.

"Mommy! Look what I found!" Nora broke away from her father and sisters to sprint across the lawn toward Meg. The ominous overcast of the morning had given way to a bright blue sky.

"That's a really pretty scallop shell, honey." Meg ran her fingers over the corrugations on the back of the shell. "It's got a little hole in the top, though."

"That's the best part!" Nora said. "I can make it into a necklace."

Jack, Marie and Daisy caught up to them. Something passed between Meg and Jack when their eyes met, a newfound depth of intimacy, as if the events of the past few days had taken their relationship to a level they hadn't known existed.

His smile was gentle. The cool autumn sunlight revealed a network of tiny lines near his eyes she'd never noticed before.

Two years was a long time.

Her heart swelled painfully with the inexhaustible love she felt for this man. Taking a deep breath, she said, "Been strolling on the beach, I see."

"The girls wanted to go down to the water one last time before we left," Jack said.

"I found a wock!" Daisy cried. "A *big* wock!"

Meg admired the smooth, amber-colored stone clutched in the little girl's chubby fingers.

"I found another piece of beach glass," Marie said, displaying the frosty shard.

"Our bags are in the living room," Meg said. "Why don't you pack these treasures so you don't forget them."

Daisy said, "I want to carry my wock on the boat."

Marie led her sisters back to the house, warning Daisy, "I'm not gonna carry it for you when you get tired." They bickered until the door closed behind them.

"Come with me." Meg slipped her arm through Jack's. "Let's walk."

They strolled across the lawn and descended the log staircase. There was no boat within sight yet, but then, it wasn't quite noon. As she recalled, the *Mermaid*'s captain was punctual. With any luck, the police would arrive promptly once they were summoned on the charter boat's radio, and wouldn't detain the party long. Meg wasn't looking forward to being questioned by the police, but she no longer dreaded it. The events of Thanksgiving night, while shocking and tragic, were indisputable.

On the beach Jack took her hand and they walked along the waterline. After a few minutes of amiable silence, he said, "I'm sorry how this turned out, Meg. I know you loved your uncle."

She sighed. "Yes. I did. I guess I always thought of Pete the way I saw him when I was growing up. Generous. Gregarious. Larger than life. The man owned an *island*, for heaven's sake. Heady stuff for a trailer-park brat like me."

"It's your island now."

She turned to look at the house, but it was obscured

from view behind the bluffs and the scrub pines. She and Jack could have been the only two people on the island at that moment.

She faced him, her hand still nestled in his. "It's ours."

He searched her face. "Yours and the girls', you mean."

"No, I mean...marry me, Jack," she whispered, trembling with emotion. "Please marry me again."

For a stunned moment he simply stared at her, unblinking. Then his hand crushed hers and those blue eyes filled. Slowly, so slowly, he pulled her into his arms, with a ragged sob that echoed her own. His arms banded around her until all she could feel was his heaving chest and his thudding heart. He lowered his head to press his cold, wet cheek to hers.

"You are my life," he whispered hoarsely, and squeezed her tighter still. "My *life!*"

She couldn't say how long they stood there entwined, anointing each other with tears of joy and relief. At last they eased apart, but he kept hold of her hands, bringing her knuckles to his lips for a lingering kiss, his eyes bright and fixed on hers.

"You haven't said yes," she teased.

"Maybe I'll make you get down on one knee and do it right."

"I'm sure you'd like that."

"And while I have you down there proposing, I might just come up with one or two propositions of my own."

Her smile was crooked. "How very romantic."

He slid his arms around her waist. "What kind of engagement ring do you want?"

"You don't have to buy me a—"

"Yes I do. I couldn't afford it the first time around, and then the counselor beat me to the diamond I always wanted to give you."

"No diamonds. Between Pete's ring and that ostentatious boulder Winston put on my finger, I don't think I could stomach the thought of another diamond."

"Words to warm any husband's heart. I'm sure we can come up with a suitable alternative. After all..." He slid his hands lower to cup her bottom and pull her to him. "We have such excellent imaginations."

His eyes, as he stared down at her, were the same shade of azure as the sky. The bay stretched out behind him, magnifying the sense of isolation. She pulled his head down and kissed him deeply, until a thick, tingling thrill shuddered through her.

He returned her kiss with a thoroughness that melted her knees. Still gripping her bottom, he moved his hips against her, ever so slightly. She moaned into his mouth and hooked one leg around his hips. He groped for the zipper pull on her anorak.

Cold air rushed in when he opened her jacket, but she didn't care because his hands were there, warming her through her shirt and then tugging it out of her waistband to glide beneath. They struggled for balance, a three-legged beast, writhing, groping, breathless.

Dropping her leg, she gasped, "We'd better stop."

"Not yet." His hand slid between her legs. The pressure was scalding, electric. "I did promise to kiss it all better, remember?"

He popped the button on her fly. Slowly pulled the zipper down. Odd little sounds came from her throat. Her body pumped in anticipation.

He knelt to drag her jeans off, giving her an unobstructed view of the bay. "Jack!" She yanked her pants up and hurriedly fastened them.

"Please don't tell me there's a boat behind me."

She scowled. "Just on time." They groaned in unison. The *Mermaid* was headed straight for the pier.

Jack stood and helped her straighten her clothing. He tucked in her shirt and zipped her jacket, snugging the collar around her throat.

"By the way, my answer is yes." He grinned. "In case there was any doubt."

_____Epilogue_____

Christmas Eve

"SO. HOW DID IT COMPARE to the first time around?"
Jack loosened his necktie and undid the top couple of
buttons on his starched dress shirt. Flopping onto his
living room sofa, he watched his bride of seven
hours—or seven years, depending how you looked at
it—kick off her high-heeled pumps.

Her wedding dress was sophisticated but alluring,
made of some filmy, pale blue material that swished
around her calves. The top was covered by a satin bro-
cade jacket of the same color, with a mandarin collar.
It went beautifully with her engagement ring: sap-
phires and emeralds in a contemporary bar pattern.

"Well, if you'll recall," she said, settling on the opposite end of the sofa and depositing her stockinged
feet in his lap, "Marie interrupted our first wedding.
Twice."

"Marie? Oh yeah." He smiled at the memory of his
sallow-faced two-months-pregnant bride dashing out
of the church sanctuary with a hand clamped over her
mouth. He'd followed her into the ladies' room to
hold back her hair and help her freshen up. Meg had

always experienced hellacious morning sickness, poor thing.

He said, "Well, at least this time nobody will be whispering that we had to get married. Not with the fruit of our loins serving as flower girls."

They'd invited about forty guests to witness their repeat nuptials. Afterward everyone had come back here to their new, half-furnished house—the big old yellow Victorian—for a buffet dinner. Kevin had suggested they hold the reception in the pub, but Jack and Meg both wanted to host it themselves, with festive hominess.

The house was swathed in pine garlands and twinkling white lights. A ten-foot-tall blue spruce stood sentry in the high-ceilinged living room, before the enormous bay window. The tree was festooned with popcorn-and-cranberry garlands, blinking multicolored lights and a wonderfully eclectic mixture of ornaments, including the girls' handmade creations. An ornate gold-and-ivory angel stared down from the summit.

Mounds of wrapped presents spilled from the tree skirt at its base. The girls' Christmas stockings hung from the carved oak mantel, awaiting Santa's bounty; they'd set out cookies and milk for him on the hearth. Jack had turned off the floor lamps after the last of the guests departed an hour ago. Between the fire that burned low in the fireplace and the twinkling colored lights reflecting off the window, the room was awash in holiday magic. The mingled seasonal aromas of good food, evergreens and a hint of wood smoke suffused the air.

Meg wiggled her toes in his lap.

He said, "You trying to tell me something?"

She whined, "I hate high heels."

He started massaging one of her feet, and she groaned in ecstasy. He asked, "Are the kids asleep?"

"Yep. All that activity, the full bellies...I was lucky to get them out of their finery and into their jammies before they conked out."

"It's going to feel strange, leaving them for a whole week."

They planned to drive down to Long Island the day after Christmas and drop the girls off with Meg's sister Laurie before catching a flight to Hawaii for their first-ever honeymoon.

"I think they'll have a ball staying with their cousins. Thank goodness Laurie has the disposition for it. She always was the mellow one." Meg stretched languorously as he switched his attention to her other foot. "I'm more concerned about the pub."

"Kevin has the number of our hotel. And you know he can handle anything."

"I know. I'm just not used to feeling so...proprietary about my work."

"We own it," he said with a chuckle. "We're supposed to feel proprietary."

Meg was in the process of selling Pete's game company in Queens, and intended to invest part of the proceeds in the Wolf Mann Brew Pub. Though both she and Jack were grateful she could now afford to stay home with their children, she insisted she wanted to get involved in the pub, on a part-time basis.

Already she'd begun educating herself about the business, and was using her marketing expertise to lay the groundwork for selling Jack and Kevin's distinctive beers in local stores. She'd contacted distributors, and the response was encouraging. She envisioned penetration of the entire Northeast within a couple of years.

When she'd finally allowed herself to get involved in the pub—specifically, when she'd begun calculating the potential of expanding into additional locations, as well as retail distribution—he'd seen that gleam come into her eye. She was hooked, infected with the heady thrill of entrepreneurship.

Jack was certain she would have embraced the business even without the financial cushion of her inheritance to fall back on. He'd seen her bravely confront her insecurities and conquer them, before becoming a wealthy woman.

He said, "I don't want you worrying about anything while we're away. The kids are in good hands and so is Wolf Mann. I want you to just relax and forget about...everything."

Her expression told him she knew what he meant by "everything." Her uncle's bizarre death still saddened her. The police had quickly come to the same conclusion Jack and Meg had about the cause of Pete's death. The autopsy had revealed that he'd suffered a massive stroke, and incurred the head wound during the fall down the stairs. He was probably dead before he reached the bottom. In the end, he'd been the victim of his own murderous rage.

Jack said, "What you need is a nice soothing bath to take your mind off everything."

The faintest of smiles lit her hazel eyes. "You going to scrub my back?"

"If you ask nicely."

Her heel lightly stroked the bulge swelling in his charcoal suit pants. "I'm asking."

"Nicely."

"Please..." she purred, climbing onto his lap with feline grace, straddling him. "Oh, please...I need you to scrub my back, I need you to get me squeaky clean...everywhere."

He felt her teasing breath as she nuzzled his throat, felt her heat and the maddening pressure of her thighs as she wriggled on his lap.

"Oh, very well." He chuckled, sliding his hands over her hips and under the satin jacket. "What does the rest of this dress look like?"

She sat up and slid the mother-of-pearl buttons free from her throat to her waist. She spread the jacket open, shimmied it off her shoulders and let it slide down her arms to the floor.

Jack whistled. "You and your little secrets." He let his hands rove up her rib cage to her breasts, snugly sheathed by the wrapped halter-neck bodice that bared her shoulders. "How does this thing open?" He reached around her and found only the satiny, warm skin of her back, exposed practically to her waist. "I *like* this dress!"

She said, "I thought it was flannel that turned you on," punctuating her statement with a gyration that told him she was well aware of the effect she had on him.

His hips moved restlessly under hers. "Maybe I should go run that bath. If the kids wake up and come down here, they're liable to see Mommy doing a whole lot more than kissing Santa Claus."

"The little darlings are out for the count. Trust me."

"And then there's that big old bay window right behind us."

She was facing that window, and now waved gaily over the back of the sofa. "It's dark in here. The tree's in the way. And anyway, all the naughty parts are hidden from view. What made you such an old stick-in-the-mud?"

He slipped his hands under her skirt and up her stocking-clad thighs. "What made you such a wild woman?"

"Two years of celibacy. I have to make up for lost time." Angling up, she unfastened his belt and his pants.

"I hate panty hose," he growled. He grabbed two handfuls of nylon and ripped the offending garment at the crotch. She gasped, and then gasped again when his fingers found her slick and ready.

"You've been walking around all day without panties?" he said, taking full advantage of that fact.

"I—I, uh...didn't want a panty line—oh!"

"Such a sensible woman." He explored her, caressed her, watching her ecstatic expression bathed in flickering colored lights. "Have I told you lately how much I appreciate your sensible side?"

"What?" she panted. "Oh, shut up."

He burrowed one finger, then two, into her hot passage. She squirmed, riding his hand, holding on to his shoulders.

"What's that you say?" he teased. "'Shut up'? You don't want me to talk? You don't want me to tell you what I'm going to do to you?"

Her eyes had that slumberous, passion-drugged look guaranteed to make him harder than portland cement. "What..." she whispered, "what are you going to do to me?"

"Uh-uh-uh, you told me to shut up."

His other hand fondled her breasts, their pointed tips jutting against the filmy cloth. He pinched a nipple lightly, then with greater pressure as she moaned and tightened around his fingers.

She smiled. "I didn't mean it. I was...overcome. Please tell me what you're going to do to me."

"I don't know. It might...shock you."

"Shock me."

He slid his fingers out of her to grasp the stiff little heart of her desire. She bucked like a wild thing. "What I have in mind," he said, "involves warm almond oil..."

"Yes...?" she panted.

"...these panty hose cut into four lengths..."

"Yes? Yes?" She writhed on his busy fingers.

"...and a bottle of nut-brown ale. Room temperature."

She blinked in surprise. In the next heartbeat her face scrunched and luscious spasms rippled through her. He released his erection and pressed into her slippery heat, in short, quick thrusts that prolonged her pleasure. Throwing back his head, he grappled for control. It was so good between them. Unbearably good.

Could he ever get enough of this woman?

At last she sagged against him, sated, mewling like a kitten. With his hands on her hips, he slowly rocked into her.

She mumbled, "What're you going to do with the cut panty hose?"

"You'll find out."

"Tell me!"

"Such impertinence. I see a little discipline is in order. Don't bother begging for mercy."

She grinned, clearly enjoying the game. "Maybe I will and maybe I won't."

"First," he said, "I'm going to bathe you. And I feel it's only fair to warn you, I intend to do incredibly depraved things to you in that big old tub upstairs."

"As long as it doesn't involve soap on a rope."

"Then I'm going to carry you into our room and tie you hand and foot to the bedposts, you impudent jezebel."

"Naked?"

"But of course."

"Oh, have mercy." Her body grasped him tightly. He groaned. "And then...?"

"Then I'm going to take that warm almond oil and rub it all over you."

"Everywhere?" Her movements took on a fresh urgency.

"Everywhere you can think of and a few places I'll bet you can't."

Her nails gouged his shoulders through his shirt. She met his quick, hard thrusts, smiling like the jezebel he'd dubbed her.

Breathless now, she asked, "The ale. What're you going to do with the ale?"

He was close now, so close, but managed a shrug. "I'm gonna drink it."

Meg laughed and came and merrily cursed him out, all at the same time. He let himself join her then, pulling her down hard, arching into her, spilling himself in a white-hot torrent.

They slumped together in a humid heap, listening to their breathing slow. A log settled in the hearth, with a hiss of sparks. Her face rested in the crook of his neck.

He smacked his lips. "I could use that ale now. You want one?"

"No. Well, yeah, but I'm not going to let myself have one."

"Don't want your senses dulled during the upcoming debauchery?" he snickered.

"You ought to know there's only one thing that can keep me from enjoying a cold beer after hot sex."

Jack took a whole three seconds to figure that one out. He jerked upright, with Meg still in his arms. Tilting her head back, he looked her in the eye. "You're not!"

She smiled.

"You are?"

"Why are you so surprised?" she asked. "Making babies is something we're real good at. I mean, we've got that one *down*."

He slouched back against the sofa, a silly grin on his face. His hand strayed to her belly, which he stroked reverently. "When do you think it happened?"

"I know when it happened. That first night, on Uncle Pete's sofa. It was so...I just know it happened then."

"Good thing we reconciled. You'd have had to marry me anyway, so I could make an honest woman of you."

"Been there, done that."

"How long have you known?"

"For sure? Since that little plus sign turned up on the home-pregnancy-test stick a few minutes ago. I've suspected for over a week, but I didn't want to verify it until after the wedding." She smiled tenderly. "I wanted this time around to be about us. Just you and me."

"Wait a minute. You can't be pregnant."

"And this is because...?" she prompted.

"You're not puking."

"Yeah, how about that!" She disengaged herself from his embrace and staggered to her feet. "No morning, afternoon and evening sickness this time. Maybe that means it's a boy."

"Boy? What's that? Sounds like some strange new life-form. Let's stick to what we know." In truth, he'd be thrilled to have a son, but if Meg gave him another wonderful little girl, he'd feel just as blessed.

He gained his feet and straightened his clothing. Sort of. She peeled off her ruined panty hose and draped them around his neck. "There," she said, "that's rather festive, don't you agree?"

"Think Santa'll leave us anything if we hang them on the mantel?"

"Speaking of which—first things first. The stockings have to be filled. And Santa has to make all gone with his cookies and milk."

"Maybe Mrs. Claus will help. Then Santa can do all those dirty things he talked about."

"She'd be a fool to refuse."

Jack pulled Meg into his arms and solemnly cupped her face. "Thank you. Thank you for marrying me again. Thank you for having my babies. Thank you for being such a good mother to them." He kissed her, trembling with emotion. "Thank you for loving me."

She dragged in an unsteady breath, her eyes shiny. "The baby, the house, my getting into the business. This really is a new beginning for us, isn't it?"

"It's as new as we want to make it."

She slid her arms around his neck and he pulled her close.

"Merry Christmas, Jack."

"Happy New Year, Meg."

She grinned. "You know, I like the sound of that."

**A showgirl, a minister—
and an unsolved murder.**

EASY VIRTUE

Eight years ago Mary Margaret's father was convicted of a violent murder she knew he didn't commit—and she vowed to clear his name. With her father serving a life sentence, Mary Margaret is working as a showgirl in Reno when Reverend Dane Barrett shows up with information about her father's case. Working to expose the real killer, the unlikely pair also proceed to expose themselves to an unknown enemy who is intent on keeping the past buried.

**From the bestselling author of
LAST NIGHT IN RIO**

JANICE
KAISER

Available in December 1997
at your favorite retail outlet.

MIRA
BOOKS

The Brightest Stars in Women's Fiction.™

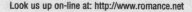

Take 4 bestselling love stories FREE

Plus get a FREE surprise gift!

Special Limited-time Offer

Mail to Harlequin Reader Service®

3010 Walden Avenue
P.O. Box 1867
Buffalo, N.Y. 14240-1867

YES! Please send me 4 free Harlequin Temptation® novels and my free surprise gift. Then send me 4 brand-new novels every month, which I will receive before they appear in bookstores. Bill me at the low price of $2.90 each plus 25¢ delivery and applicable sales tax, if any.* That's the complete price and a savings of over 10% off the cover prices—quite a bargain! I understand that accepting the books and gift places me under no obligation ever to buy any books. I can always return a shipment and cancel at any time. Even if I never buy another book from Harlequin, the 4 free books and the surprise gift are mine to keep forever.

142 BPA A3UP

Name	(PLEASE PRINT)	
Address	Apt. No.	
City	State	Zip

This offer is limited to one order per household and not valid to present Harlequin Temptation® subscribers. *Terms and prices are subject to change without notice. Sales tax applicable in N.Y.

UTEMP-696   ©1990 Harlequin Enterprises Limited

Look what Santa brought!

CHRISTMAS DELIVERY

Capture the holiday spirit with these three
heartwarming stories of moms, dads,
babies and mistletoe. *Christmas Delivery*
is the perfect stocking stuffer featuring three
of your favorite authors:

A CHRISTMAS MARRIAGE by Dallas Schulze
DEAR SANTA by Margaret St. George
THREE WAIFS AND A DADDY by Margot Dalton

**There's always room for one more—
especially at Christmas!**

Available wherever Harlequin and Silhouette
books are sold.

CHRISTMAS MIRACLES

really can happen, and Christmas dreams can come true!

BETTY NEELS,
Carole Mortimer and Rebecca Winters

bring you the magic of Christmas in this wonderful holiday collection of romantic stories intertwined with Christmas dreams come true.

Join three of your favorite romance authors as they celebrate the festive season in their own special style!

Available in November at your favorite retail store.

HARLEQUIN®

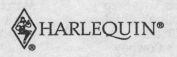

DEBBIE MACOMBER

invites you to the

HEART OF TEXAS

Join Debbie Macomber as she brings you the lives
and loves of the folks in the ranching community
of Promise, Texas.

If you loved Midnight Sons—don't miss
Heart of Texas! A brand-new six-book series
from Debbie Macomber.

Available in February 1998
at your favorite retail store.

Heart of Texas by Debbie Macomber

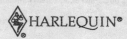

HARLEQUIN®

HPHRT1

As Seen on TV!

Free Gift Offer

With a Free Gift proof-of-purchase
from any Harlequin® book, you can receive
a beautiful cubic zirconia pendant.

This stunning marquise-shaped stone is a genuine cubic
zirconia—accented by an 18" gold tone necklace.
(Approximate retail value $19.95)

Send for yours today...
compliments of ◈HARLEQUIN®

To receive your free gift, a cubic zirconia pendant, send us one original proof-of-
purchase, photocopies not accepted, from the back of any Harlequin Romance®,
Harlequin Presents®, Harlequin Temptation®, Harlequin Superromance®, Harlequin
Intrigue®, Harlequin American Romance®, or Harlequin Historicals® title available at
your favorite retail outlet, together with the Free Gift Certificate, plus a check or money
order for $1.65 u.s./$2.15 can. (do not send cash) to cover postage and handling,
payable to Harlequin Free Gift Offer. We will send you the specified gift. Allow 6 to
8 weeks for delivery. Offer good until December 31, 1997, or while quantities last. Offer
valid in the U.S. and Canada only.

Free Gift Certificate

Name: _____

Address: _____

City: _____ State/Province: _____ Zip/Postal Code: _____

Mail this certificate, one proof-of-purchase and a check or money order for postage
and handling to: HARLEQUIN FREE GIFT OFFER 1997. In the U.S.: 3010 Walden
Avenue, P.O. Box 9071, Buffalo NY 14269-9057. In Canada: P.O. Box 604, Fort Erie,
Ontario L2Z 5X3.

FREE GIFT OFFER   084-KEZ

ONE PROOF-OF-PURCHASE

To collect your fabulous FREE GIFT, a cubic zirconia pendant, you must include this
original proof-of-purchase for each gift with the properly completed Free Gift Certificate.

084-KEZR